Midnight Blood

The Beginning of Forever

Nicole L Yanski

Released June 2012

The characters and events portrayed in this book are fictitious. Any
similarity to places, and people, living or dead, is coincidental or
used in a fictitious way by the author.

Born Immortal: Midnight Blood
The Beginning of Forever; a novel by Nicole L. Yanski

Summary: When Shayna is suddenly thrust into a world she never
knew existed, until she found a mysterious letter from her dead
father, she must figure out if Cain's secrets will kill her or break
her heart...or both.

ISBN: 9781475024029

BORN IMMORTAL SERIES:
Midnight Blood: The Beginning of Forever
Cimmerian Utopia: A New Beginning
Keeper of My Soul: For All Eternity

DEDICATED
to
My mother, who is missed every day
and to Timothy R. Hoffman, who was always a great
friend to me.
And to Luana and Cassandra,
without you two, the Born Immortal Series might not
have happened, or come this far.
I love you both.
To my husband and my children
for their support and input, and for putting up with me
through the process

Midnight Blood
By:
Nicole L Yanski

Life is eternal; and love is immortal;
and death is only a horizon;
and a horizon is nothing save the limit of our sight.

Rossiter W. Raymond

PROLOGUE

The dull red glow, surrounded by bright white, was blinding to Shayna. Her eyes fluttered open, and slowly they began to adjust to the light. She looked around, barely able to move her head. Unbelievably, she was back on the island. This time, instead of roses, there were white candles, burning through out the room. She realized that the flames from the candles, were the red glow. Everything had gone horribly wrong. Her head was pounding, and she hopelessly wondered, where Aiden was. He was supposed to protect her from Cain, to stop this from happening, and make sure it didn't happen at all.

A dark figure stepped into the room from the balcony, and walked toward the bed.

"You're awake," he said, and sat on the bed beside her.

He put his hand on her thigh, and Shayna trembled with fear. The only thing going through her mind, was that Aiden was supposed to protect her from this. She had trusted that he would do that.

"Don't be scared Shayna," he whispered to her.

He leaned down toward her, and with his soft, but deadly, fingers, he gently moved the hair off of her shoulder, exposing her throat. The veins in her neck throbbed with every beat of her heart. Right there. He thought, eyeing the biggest vein.

"This won't hurt much." He leaned in even closer to her, "If you don't fight it."

Shayna closed her eyes tightly.This is it. She thought. This is how I am going to die.

Chapter 1

Melina Verona knocked on her twin sister Shayna's bedroom door, and huffed,

"Shay, lets go, I don't want to be late."

Melina could hear her sister stirring on the other side of the door, and she grew more anxious.

"I'm up," Shayna groaned.

Shayna didn't want to wake up. She wanted so badly to go back to sleep, so that she could see *him*. The mysterious handsome boy that had been visiting her dreams for the last three years. She doesn't understand the meaning of this boy in her dreams, but she feels deep inside that he symbolizes her father. When the boy appears he doesn't ever speak, and he doesn't really play a role in her dreams. He's just there. Watching her, standing behind a tree, or walking down the street. Sometimes his beautiful face appears in the clouds looking down at her.

She had been closer than ever to him this time. He was sitting in her favorite coffee shop when she walked in. When she approached him, he held out his hand to her with a gorgeous smile, and *that* was when the knocking began.

Shayna opened her eyes and realized she was awake. Her heart sank to her stomach. She hated that feeling.

She had been so close. She didn't like leaving him, especially not this time.

"I'm up," she mumbled again. Sitting up in her bed she looked out the window. It was a nice day, it was winter but it hadn't been that cold yet. For northern Michigan the winter had been unusually mild.

Shayna rolled out of the bed and went to her bathroom to wash up, for the day, which she was not looking forward to. It was the first day back to school after Christmas break, and almost every girl in school was anxiously awaiting their return. During the break a woman and a boy, who appeared to be high school age, moved to Interlochen. The woman came to town to run errands occasionally. But the boy was only seen when people drove past their house, which was two or three miles south of town.

Shayna laughed out loud to herself when she thought of how, almost every available girl at the Interlochen Center for the Arts would be doing everything they possibly could, to catch the eye of this new stranger.

So fake. She thought. She pulled a brown hooded cardigan, and an old pair of blue jeans out of her closet. She felt like school had become more of a drama filled fashion show, than it was a learning institution. She couldn't wait to be in New York in the fall. To start her new life, to be a new Shayna.

She put on the jeans, and pulled the cardigan over the white camisole that she was already wearing. She gave her hair a quick comb over, then pulled the top half loosely back and clipped it, letting the rest of her thick chocolate curls fall over her shoulders.

She was ready. No makeup. No hairspray. Just Shayna.

Shayna grabbed her backpack, and opened her bedroom door. Standing there was Melina, arm raised in a knocking position.

"It's about time," Melina barked, "Can we go?"

"Can I eat?"

"No, I have to hurry."

"Oh puhlease." Shayna rolled her eyes.

"Grab an apple." Melina looked at her sister pathetically, and they walked down the stairs. "Come on Shay, you know the rules, 'whoever sees him first'. I have to see him first."

Shayna sat down to put on her boots, and finally took a good look at what Melina was wearing, and shook her head at the outfit.

"What?" demanded Melina, when she noticed.

"If Mom sees you wearing that she's going to freak," Shayna said, and laced up a pair of brown, leather boots, that seemed to be very worn out.

Melina wore a white blouse, a pink floral skirt, that by Shayna's standards was too short, and a pair of white almost knee high boots.

"Mom's not going to see me, Miss Perfect," Melina responded, then whispered, "Now lets go, before she wakes up."

Shayna rolled her eyes again and stood up from the bench that was at their back door, "Lets go."

They walked to the car, and Shayna knew inside, that the day would be good. She had an odd feeling that something was going to happen. Then she remembered that something *was* going to happen today. This new boy, though no one was quite sure of his name, should be at school today. He would join the few locals that attended the Academy, but she couldn't figure out why *she* would feel anxious about that.

On the way to school Melina talked Shayna's ear off about the new boy. Wondering what he looked like, if he was cute, how old he was, blah, blah, blah. Shayna wanted to hum along with the sound of their Honda Prelude's motor, and tune her sister out.

"You know, your whole 'whoever sees him first' rule is childish," Shayna finally said to Melina, "You're interfering with fate."

"Who is to say we all even like him," Melina defended, "That rule is just in case more than one of us like a guy. Whoever saw him first gets the first shot."

"Obviously," Shayna said, and glared at her sister.

"Whatever Shayna." Melina was getting more defensive, "We're not interfering with anybody's fate!"

Just his. Shayna thought, and looked out the window. She was silent the rest of the way to school. She wished she was still dreaming.

Melina and Shayna are fraternal twins. They live in a small northern Michigan village with their mother Sarah. Their father, Marcus, died when they were thirteen. They are now half way through their senior year in high school, and will both be going to college in the fall. Melina to Michigan State, and Shayna to New York.

Calling them unidentical twins is an understatement. They are worlds apart. Melina, with fine straight blond hair, brown eyes, thin lips, and a medium build, like their mother. Shayna with chocolate curly hair, big bright blue eyes, and full kissable lips, like their father. Although no one is quite sure where Shayna got her petite body from. To top it off their personalities are polar opposites. Melina is obsessed with her looks, boys, and material objects, and Shayna likes art, reading, and being in nature. Most people don't even believe that the girls are sisters, let alone twins.

~ 4 ~

They pulled into the student parking lot almost a half an hour early.

"I'm going across the street to the coffee shop," Shayna told Melina, when the car was parked. This was the coffee shop in her dream. "Good luck…with your…thing."

"Okay, see ya," Melina said over her shoulder. She was already out of the car and on her way.

Shayna got out of the car and took a deep breath. The air was cool and crisp. It felt more like fall than winter. She walked across the street to the coffee shop. Inside was a kid that she had gone to school with forever, but could never remember his name, a couple of freshmen cheerleaders, and Evan, an attractive boy from Italy, who was always oddly staring at Shayna. But, no dream boy. Shayna knew she was silly for even thinking he would be there for real. She ordered a white chocolate mocha and a banana nut muffin, and walked outside and sat at a table to read. She was reading *Utopia* by Sir Thomas More. She had found it two years earlier, along with a couple of other valuable and sentimental keepsakes of her father's, in their attic.

She was just opening the book when she heard the sound of a fast car approaching.

She looked up. Was this the new boy? She watched as the black BMW whipped around the corner, and into the school parking lot. When he was out of the car he was too far away from her, for her to get a good look at him. She could tell he had shoulder length hair that was the same color as hers, and that he was dressed all in black.

"Here we go," she mumbled to herself.

There was no doubt in Shayna's mind that Melina would see this boy before Delany and Maria, her two best friends. Maria rode the bus, and Delany refused to get out of bed early for a boy, even if she *did* live at the school. So as long as he arrived early enough, which he did, Melina was gauranteed to see him first.

The boy approached the doors to the office, and reaching to open them, he stopped and turned around, and looked right at Shayna sitting across the street at the coffee shop. Shayna quickly looked back down at *Utopia*. She could not see his eyes when he looked at her, but she could feel them. Had he felt *her* looking at him too? That's ridiculous. She thought, and peeked back up, he was gone.

Shayna walked into the school, and to her surprise, Melina and Maria were standing by the inside doors to the office, boyless and looking flustered. Shayna smiled to herself, and walked down the hall to the Biology Lab. She would have to ask Melina at lunch what had happened, she found herself interested to know.

The rest of the morning her thoughts were on the new boy. The lunch bell rang and she all but ran to Melina's locker. She knew Melina would be there, she always went there before meeting her "girls". She rounded the corner to the hall Melina's locker was in, and like clockwork there was Melina.

"Well?" she asked, walking up to her sister.

"Don't even ask." Melina glared, but proceeded anyway, "When I got to the office, Marie was already there, she had her Host Mom drop her off. After he checked in, we both offered to show him around, and he said 'No thank you', can you believe that?"

Shayna laughed, "He rejected you?"

"It's not funny Shayna." She glared, this time it was directed *at* Shayna.

"Sorry, but how many times can your little 'welcome wagon' plan work before your friends catch on?" Shayna said, her lips curling into a smile. "It is a little funny."

"Whatever. I'll meet you at the car at 3:15," Melina said, and she stormed off.

After lunch, Shayna had Advanced Art, she left the cafeteria, and headed to the other side of the campus. She walked in the classroom, sat down and pulled her sketch book out of her backpack.

"It's good to see everyone," Ms. Olson said greeting the class, after the bell had rang.

Ms. Olson was the epitomy of 'Hippie', and very cool. Shayna thought she smoked marijuana, but wasn't sure. She was wearing a tie dye skirt, a purple blouse, and Birkenstock sandals. Her frizzy hair was put up in a messy bun, on top of her head.

"Welcome back. Today we're going t..." she began, but was interrupted by the door opening, and a boy dressed all in black walked in. He walked to Ms.Olson and gave her his enrollment slip for the office. This was the new boy. Shayna could not believe how handsome he was. Dark and handsome.

"You must be Cain," Ms. Olson said, reaching for the slip. He nodded his head, not taking his eyes off of the woman. " You may take a seat in the back next to Shayna," she said after a second.

Shayna looked up as Ms. Olson pointed in her direction, and she and this boy, Cain, made eye contact. It was a good thing she was sitting down, because her knees went weak when he looked at her. Thoughts raced through her mind. She tried to figure out why she was feeling this way. All she knew, was that she couldn't take her eyes off of him. He was absolutly gorgeous, he had shoulder length wavy dark hair, a tall broad build and the most beautiful green eyes she had ever seen. He looked like a model for a men's magazine. No wonder he didn't accept Melina and Maria's gesture, he was way out of their league. He seemed more sophisticated and mature, then most of the girls at the Center for the Arts.

Their eyes stayed locked as he sauntered down the aisle toward her. He smiled and he sat down, outstretching his hand to her.

"Cain," he said, hand open to shake hers.

Shayna flashed him a smile and waved his hand away, "Shayna," she replied.

"Okay, guys," Ms.Olson said over the whispering, which no doubt was about Cain. "I know how much everyone likes Still Lifes drawings, so I thought that we would start the New Year off with one." She gestured to a table that had a variety of items on it, like, wine bottles, vases with flowers, old cigar boxes. Even the skull of a bull. "If everyone would choose a place around the table, and take a seat, we can begin."

The students got up, and found where they would sit. Cain was sitting behind Shayna and to her right. As she drew, she felt the same feeling of his eyes on her, as she had when he had looked at her from across the street. Why did she blow him off like that? She could have at least shaken his hand.

She couldn't stop thinking about his eyes, as she drew. Maybe that is why she thought he was staring at her. She finally got the courage to look over her shoulder at him. He was staring at her! She quickly looked back to her sketch book. Why was he looking at her? She thought. And why so intently?

This went on throughout the rest of the class she would sneak casual peaks at him, out of the corner of her eye, and most of the time he was watching her. What is going on? she kept wondering.

Ms. Olson dismissed the class and Shayna gathered her things and headed for the door, but stopped in her steps when she heard a soft, musical voice say her name. Her knees weakened a little. She turned to face him.

"Yes?" She tried to act casually, although her heart was pounding in her chest. What was going on with her? She couldn't help but wonder.

"Can you help me find my next class?" he asked, with a smile that made his green eyes more beautiful.

Are you serious? She thought.

"Sure," she tried the casual thing again. This boy had refused the 'welcome wagon' of one of the most beautiful girls in school, her twin sister, and he was asking Shayna for help. "What is your next class?"

"World History, with Mr. Duncan," he answered.

"Okay" she said, and they walked out of the art room together. "You're going to go down the hall, take a left and go all the way down, last door on the right."

He looked at her and smiled, "Thank you Shayna," and he turned and walked away.

Hearing him say her name again, gave her chills, and she began to feel dizzy. Shayna watched him walk away. He turned the corner, and looked back and smiled at her again. Like he knew she was watching him. She didn't move until another student bumped into her from behind. She was kind of in shock. Her mind was racing with thoughts about this new boy. Thoughts she refused to let herself think about the other boys she went to school with. She wondered why he had asked *her* for directions. He could have asked any of the other kids in the class. But he chose, probably, the only girl who didn't throw herself at his feet, and she wouldn't even shake his hand. What is wrong with you? She scolded herself.

Maybe that was it, he saw through all their hairdye and makeup, and saw what was underneath. Maybe she should be flattered. Then she thought of Melina. Melina was after this boy, so she would have to keep any thoughts she had about him to herself. That wouldn't be hard to do. Shayna kept a lot of things from her twin. She has never told Melina about the boy she dreams about. Melina would just laugh at her, and tell her to get a boyfriend. She also hasn't told Melina what she found in the attic two years earlier.

When the final bell rang at 3:10 Shayna felt like she couldn't get out of the school building fast enough. She just wanted to go home. She got to the Honda, and Melina wasn't there yet. Big surprise, Shayna thought. She reached in her bag for her set of keys but came up empty. Melina and Shanya share the Honda Prelude, but Melina drives mostly. Shayna remembered that her keys were sitting on her dresser at home. She leaned against the car and began thinking about Cain. She couldn't stop thinking about his eyes. They were so alluring, and so green. She had never seen eyes that color of green before. They were the color of emeralds. Bright sparkling green.

Melina showed up around 3:30, late as always, and Shayna realized that Cain's BMW was already gone. When had he left? Was his car there when she came outside? She couldn't remember. She had been too busy thinking about him, to even think to see if he had left.

"Sorry I'm late," Melina apologized and unlocked the door, "The girls and I had to exchange notes."

"What did you find out?" Shayna asked to fulfill her own curiosity, and climbed into the car.

"Nothing really," Melina plopped into the driver seat and threw her bag in the back seat. "He really didn't talk to anyone but Noah, I heard he lives with his aunt though."

Melina had caught Shayna's attention, "Noah? Why was he talking to Noah?" she asked her.

Noah was the one person that didn't totally repulse Shayna, at the Art Academy. He was the only person that she was close to, and trusted.

"I don't know," Melina responded. "Delany saw them talking in Gym. She couldn't hear them."

Shayna looked out the window, "Oh," she said.

"Why do you care?" Melina asked.

"I don't," Shayna said, turning her head quickly back to face Melina. "I was just wondering why he was talking to Noah is all."

"Why not Noah, *everyone* talks to Noah. Shay are you okay?" Melina looked at Shayna quizzically.

"I'm fine," she laughed, "I was just curious."

"Well anyways," Melina went on. "I'm not sure what to do. I don't know anything about him, so I don't know where to start, and Maria said I can have him, she said it would be pointless, and wished me luck." Melina laughed, and ran her fingers through her golden locks. "Like I need it."

"Oh brother," Shayna rolled her eyes. "Just give him time and space, it's his first day of school, maybe he's shy."

"Did you see him?" Shayna nodded in response to Melina's question, and Melina continued, "Did you see those eyes?" Melina didn't wait for the answer, "He is definitely not shy!"

Shayna thought about those eyes. She couldn't stop thinking about them. So green and captivating. She'd only seen eyes that beautiful, in her dreams. Did they have the same eyes? No, *his* were blue. She shook the thought out of her head.

When they pulled onto Melody Lane, Shayna saw their mothers Jeep in their driveway before Melina did, and smiled.

"Oh crap," Melina blurted out, and turned around in her seat while driving, and looked in the backseat for something to change into fast, but for the first time, the Honda had nothing, Shayna had cleaned it out the weekend before. She looked at Shayna pleadingly, "Tell mom I'm going back, to hang out with Delany, and I'll be back for dinner."

"Going to change your clothes?" Shayna asked grinning.

"She wasn't supposed to be here tonight," Melina told her, "I checked the chart."

"Tell Delany 'Hi' for me," Shayna said sarcastically and got out of the car.

"Thanks Shay."

Shayna winked at her, "You owe me." She closed the car door, and bound up the walkway to the house and opened front door.

"Mom," she shouted. She was concerned, she hoped she wasn't ill. "Where are you?"

"In the kitchen Shay," she heard her mother answer. Shayna walked into the kitchen.

"I thought you were working today," she said to her mother.

"I'm on call, I just put it on the fridge chart so you girls weren't expecting me home," Sarah Verona works nights at Munson Medical Center as a phlebotomist. She had been there since she graduated twenty years earlier. Their father Marcus had supported their mother, and had taken care of the girls so that she could go back to work. "So far no call," she smiled at her daughter, "So how was the new boy? Was he worth all the fuss?"

Shayna smiled and said, "Probably. He seems to be keeping to himself, and I think that's causing a bigger fuss."

"What do you mean?" Sarah asked.

"I don't know, he hasn't really talked to anyone, and I think it's driving some of the girls crazy. Most of them aren't used to being ignored." Shayna twisted the ends of her hair.

"Ah, I see," Sarah put her hands on Shayna's, "I bet he didn't ignore you."

Shayna looked at her mom, her eyes were tired and full of love for her daughter. "How do you know?" she shook her head, and narrowed her eyes.

"You're beautiful Shayna," she squeezed her hand, "You don't need blonde hair dye, and gobs of make up. You're naturally beautiful. Do I have to tell you that everyday?"

"No, I guess not," she sighed.

She did know she was beautiful. She just didn't care. She knew that every boy at school wanted her, and she knew that it drove them crazy that she wouldn't have them.

"He only asked me for directions to his next class, no big deal," she smiled at Sarah, "I love you Mom."

"I love you too Shayna," she gave Shayna a hug, kissed her forehead and said, "I'm going upstairs to take a nap in case I do get called in."

"Okay," Shayna said and grabbed her backpack. "I'm going to go for a walk."

"Just be back by seven for dinner," Sarah said, heading up the stairs.

Shayna grabbed an apple off the counter, and headed upstairs herself, eating as she walked. She went into her room, and threw her backpack on her bed, grabbed her art bag, and headed back down. She threw the apple in the garbage on her way out the door, and walked toward the edge of the forest, where their path was. The path had been there for years. Permanantly beaten into the ground by Melina and Shayna over time.

Shayna felt so at peace in the woods, away from the house and the town. She only had to walk about a mile in, until she got to the river. This time of year their favorite summer time creek was a raging torrent, and the waterfall was amazing. She entered the clearing and found her spot. Shayna was in the middle of a personal art project. She was drawing the waterfall in different stages of the seasons. Although there wasn't any snow to draw at the time, the waterfall still raged. She was mezmerized by how it could go from, something so calm and peaceful to a raging killer, in just a few months. She felt one with the waterfall. She was changing too.

High up in a very large maple tree, a silent, dark figure watched Shayna drawing. He couldn't take his eyes off her. She was the most magnificent creature he had ever seen. Her scent was so sweet and powerful. He licked his lips and ran his tongue over his teeth feeling the sharpness extend.

Shayna had an eerie feeling come over her. A feeling like she was being watched. She looked up to the trees, the dark figure hugged the big tree, to hide himself, and Shayna saw nothing. She remembered something her father had told her about cougars, or mountain lions, or whatever. Something about being able to feel them hunting you. The hairs on the back of her neck began to stand up, and she shivered. The DNR had confirmed Mountain Lions were *in fact* inhabiting northern Michigan. She decided it was time to go. She had never had that feeling here before....or anywhere for that matter.

It was dark when Shayna emerged from the woods. She could hear music coming from Melina's bedroom. She was already home. She opened the back door and an aroma of tomatoes, and basils, and her mother's secret ingredient filled her nostrils. Sarah kept the secret ingredient locked in an icebox in the basement. Shayna knew what was inside, but she never told her mother's secret. It was her secret too. Sarah didn't even know she knew.

"Smells good," she told Sarah, entering the kitchen.

"Thank you," Sarah smiled at her, "Will you call down Mel, it's almost done."

Shayna went to the back stairs. "Mel," she yelled, "Dinner!"

"Coming!" was the response that was yelled back.

Shayna went to the cupboard, and got the plates to set the table.

"How is your project coming Shay?" Sarah inquired.

"Good." Shayna answered. "Beside the fact, of not much snow this year, but I can still capture the waterfall. I can't wait until spring is over and I can draw the final stage.

"Mmm, I can't wait to see it," Sarah replied.

Shayna never showed anyone an unfinished project. She felt it was bad luck.

"Smells great mom," Melina said, thundering down the stairs.

The two girls sat down at the table in the dining room and Sarah brought the food in. She placed the spaghetti and garlic bread on the table and headed back to the kitchen. The smells of the food seemed overpowering to Shayna, it smelled so delicious.

"Is your registration for NYU completed and ready for this fall?" Sarah asked when she returned.

"Almost." Shayna swallowed a bite of spaghetti, "I still have to send in my transcripts."

"And when are you doing that?"

"Mrs.Wade in the office told me she would have everything ready for me by the end of the week," Shayna smiled.

"Just can't wait to get out of here can you?" Melina accused.

"Like you would miss me!" Shayna said teasingly.

"Shay," Melina looked at her sister. "Just because you're boring, and we don't hang out, doesn't mean I won't miss you."

"Awe shucks, Mel," Shayna pretended to be embarassed by her sisters sincerity, and smiled, "You're a peach."

They talked about the girls plans for college the rest of dinner. Melina had plans to go to Michigan State University to major in Journalism. She loved gossip. Shayna was going to New York University to major in art. She wanted to illustrate novel covers. They weren't like most students at the Art Acadamy, most of the students weren't even from Michigan, let alone the US. Shayna and Melina never understood why they had to attend the academy, but their father had insisted.

When dinner was over, Melina went to the living room, and sprawled out on the couch, remote control in hand. Shayna helped Sarah clean up the kitchen. They worked in silence, Shayna too busy thinking about Cain to start a conversation, and Sarah sensing Shayna in deep thought, and not wanting to interrupt.

When they were done, Shayna went upstairs to run herself a bath. She went to her room, and grabbed *Utopia* out of her backpack and her robe and went to the bathroom. She turned on the water and poured some vanilla oil in the water, and lit an incense stick. The incense seemed stronger than ever to her tonight, everything smelled stronger to her tonight. Was the change already happening? She thought. Is this part of it? Shayna took off her clothes and slid into the big clawfoot tub. She left *Utopia* on her robe on the bathroom floor, and sank back, closing her eyes.

The creek babbled over the waterfall, splashing onto the rocks below. It was spring. Shayna had come to the waterfall to be alone and think about her father. He was missing everything. Her eighteenth birthday, graduation. Everything. A tear fell down her cheek. He had written in the letter she found in *Utopia* two years earlier, that he would return to her before her eighteenth birthday. If he didn't then he was truly dead. She would be in this alone.

Suddenly a familiar feeling swept through her. She looked up to the top of the waterfall. There he was, not her father, but her dream boy. Standing at the top of the waterfall smiling down at her. She stepped towards him, and he started to walk down the jagged path next to the waterfall, toward her. As he got closer he held out his hand to her. He was so beautiful. She couldn't believe this was happening. She slowly reached her hand out to him waiting for the touch.

"Shayna," she heard from above, right as their fingertips were about to touch.

She recognized that voice, a different voice, a soft and musical voice. She looked up again to the waterfall. It *was* Cain. What was he doing here? What was going on? With his eyes, he smiled down at her. Her heart melted, and her stomach swam.

"Shayna," he said once again. Her name sounded beautiful when he said it. She remembered the other boy and looked back to him. To her dismay, he was gone. She couldn't believe she lost her opportunity to to feel his touch. She had waited so long. She didn't care if it was just a dream. Why had she been getting so close to him now? She thought. She returned her gaze up to Cain. He smiled at her and whispered, "I'm here for you now." She could not look away from his eyes, she almost felt like she was in a trance, they were so mezmerizing. He said her name again, but it was another voice that came out of his lips.

"Shayna." It was Sarah, "Are you alive in there?"
Her eyes slowly opened. She had fallen asleep in the bath, and the water was freezing. She shivered.
"I'm alive," she said through the door. "Barely," she added.
She heard her mom laugh on the other side of the door. "Good night sweetie. I'm going to bed."
"I'm getting out," Shayna told her, and pushed herself up and out of the cold water. "Good night." Shayna wrapped herself in a towel and stepped out of the bathtub, careful not to drip water on *Utopia*. She dried off and put on her robe, brushed her teeth, and went to her room. She stuffed *Utopia* into her backpack and put her pajamas on, which consisted of, a pair of flannel pants, and a t-shirt.
She grabbed her brush and started brushing her long thick hair. She couldn't stop thinking about what Cain had said. "I'm here for you now." What did that mean? Shayna put the brush back on the vanity and turned off the light and went to bed. She slept dreamless all night.

Chapter 2

***

Cain entered the meadow that morning as dawn broke, and was not surprised to see the huge hawk on a downed tree on the otherside. He knew it was already there.

Cain glared. *Well, well.* He projected. *Definitely not surprised to see you, just surprised it's so soon*

He heard the hawk's voice in his head, it was a familiar voice. *She's stronger and more pure than the rest, I'll do whatever it takes to keep you away from her.*

She will be mine fool! Cain slowly took a step forward. *You won't stop me.*

Then so be it. The hawk yelled in Cain's head. *I will stop you.* The huge hawk outstretched his wings, and lifted off the ground, and into the sky toward Cain. Cain watched as the hawk headed right for him. He ducked as it swooped down toward him, then lifted higher and was gone over the tall trees.

Crap, this isn't going to be easy. Cain told himself.

***

Shayna felt different when she woke up. She was anxious to get to school, and she couldn't believe why. Cain was the first thing she thought about when she woke up, and for the first time in three years she wanted to stay awake. There was a different boy she wanted to see today.

Shayna had a hard time accepting that she could not stop thinking about Cain. There was only one boy she ever wanted to know so much about, and he wasn't real. Cain was. She still had thoughts of her dream in the bathtub, and what he had said. *I'm here for you now.* He was here now. He was real, and she couldn't stop thinking about him.

She went to her closet and pulled out a brand new pair of jeans she got for Christmas, and put them on, she loved the way they made her butt look, which is why she never wore them. She put on a red camisole, and pulled a red silken blouse over it. She looked in the mirror that was on the back of her bedroom door.

Sarah was right, she was beautiful. She had her father's strong Roman features. His mouth, and eyes, and thick curly chocolate hair.

Why was she so stubborn? She could have any boy she wanted. She refused to be like the other girls at the academy, and use her looks, instead of talent, to get her through life. She wanted to be herself, as long as she was still herself. The exact opposite of the other girls. But yet she found herself in front of the mirror examining her outfit and hair.

She wanted to be disgusted with herself, but only saw Cain's face. She wanted to tell him she was sorry for being so rude to him. She wanted to pour her heart out to him, and tell him all of her secrets that she never told anyone else. This did disgust her! She didn't know anything about him. She wondered how she could feel this way about a stranger. Could he ever accept what I am? She thought. Anxiety swept through her again. She needed to see him. She grabbed her backpack, and ran downstairs, expecting Melina to be waiting in the kitchen for her. No Melina. Shayna looked out the living room window, and saw the Honda sitting in the driveway.

Weird. Shayna thought. She ran back upstairs, and knocked on Melina's door,

"Mel," she said, "Are you coming?"

She could hear Melina moving around on the other side of the door, and then she opened the door, "What?"

"Are you coming?" Shayna asked again.

"No," she said, "Take the car."

Shayna hated driving, "Nah, it's not bad outside. I think I'll walk."

Most of the students that attended the Interlochen Center for the Arts lived at the academy, and we're not from Interlochen or northern Michigan. Shayna was lucky, she could enjoy walking to school.

"Whatever," Melina looked at her twin, "You're really going to walk?"

"Sure," Shayna replied, "I better enjoy the nice weather while it lasts."

"Won't be long," Melina told her, and closed the door.

She went downtairs and put her boots on. She couldn't let her secrets keep her from being happy anymore. She wanted to know more about Cain. He intrigued her. She was anxious again.

She left the house, and clouds covered the sun, casting a shadow over Melody Lane. So much for a decent day. She turned onto Innwood, and an eerie feeling crept through her. The feeling from the previous night, when she felt like she was being watched. A branch broke high above her. Startled, she jumped, and looked up. A massive hawk flapped his wings in the tree above.

Shayna walked below, and the hawk watched her intently. She thought he looked larger than a normal hawk , she couldn't get over how big he appeared. High up in the tree he seemed as big as a large eagle.

The clouds cleared and the sun pierced Shayna's eyes, blinding her. When her vision was clear and she could see again, she looked back up, but the beautiful creature was gone. How odd, she pondered. She hadn't even heard him take off. She wondered if she would have heard him.

She continued to school, shrugging off the thought of the hawk. She passed by an old closed down retail shop and noticed something new. There was a sign in the window.

Grand Opening
January 4th
'Between the Lines' Bookstore and Gift Shop

She peered in the window. It looked inviting, and very comfortable inside. She took a mental note, to come back and browse around sometime. She hadn't known Interlochen was even getting a new book store.

Shayna felt a sense of ease and relief as she walked to school. She told herself that it was time to accept the change that was beginning in her life. If she had secrets that she had no control over, then she was going to have to deal with them. She thought of her father and smiled. She knew that she had meant a lot to him. Marcus Verona had loved his twin daughters equally, but Shayna was different. She was special, and she and her father were connected in a way that he and Melina were not.

Shayna knew that something inside of her had changed overnight. She could still not fathom why she felt so strongly for this new boy. Maybe it's part of the change. She thought, and wondered if her emotions and way of thinking would change too.

The art academy came into view, and Shayna thought of Melina.

What am I doing? Shayna wondered if she should tell her sister how she was feeling about Cain. She wondered if Melina would even care because, she "saw him first". The rule *didn't* apply to the twins, but Melina could be pretty selfish sometimes.

She tried to tell herself that she shouldn't pursue Cain. When she thought of Melina upset with her over a boy, she felt embarrassed. She couldn't betray her sister, even if the two twins barely knew each other anymore. But as student after student passed her on the side walk in front of the school, she found herself searching for his face amongst them.

First period felt like it dragged on. She could not wait to get out of there. She had to talk to Noah about Cain. She hoped he knew something, *anything* about him. She decided in class to tell Melina that she had an attraction to Cain. She didn't know what would happen. She didn't care. For God's sake, neither one of them even knew him!

When the bell rang she darted out of the biology lab, and went for the stairs, almost running into Derrick Jones at the top. He grabbed her as she stumbled backwards.

"Sorry," she smiled apologetically, "In a hurry."

Derrick laughed, "Yeah, I can see that."

Shayna pushed passed him and continued down the hall. Derrick had been Melina's last victim. He was a nice good looking boy, but not someone Shayna saw her sister with anyway. Shayna felt sorry for Derrick though. He had been new in the fall, and Melina played her little "Welcome Wagon" game, as always, and they had hooked up. But, Melina dropped him like a bad habit, right after Christmas, when she found out about Cain moving to Interlochen. Melina disappointed her sister sometimes, Shayna knew that she would never find love and happiness, that way.

Shayna had sent Noah a message telling him to meet her in class early. She walked into the Calculus room, and Noah was there waiting for her. She saw him and smiled.

"What's up?" he asked her. Shayna wanted a chance to talk to him before class. She sat down.

"You meet the new guy?" she asked.

"Yeah. He seems cool," Noah said, and leaned back in his chair. Shayna loved being around him. He made her laugh,and he never tried to impress people either. He refused to care about what people thought. He was a lot more sociable than Shayna though. Sitting there with a fedora on his head, covering his flat brown hair, and Converses on his feet, she couldn't help but laugh.

"What?" he didn't get it.

"Nothing," she said, and pulled all of her long curls around her neck to one side, "What do you know about him?"

"What do you want to know?" he asked her in a joking tone, and then realized, that Shayna wants to know about a guy! "Wait what?" he demanded suspiciously.

She couldn't make eye contact with him, and turned her head away, "I'm curious, is all"

Noah leaned closer to her, and caught her face and turned it towards his, "Cut the crap, Shayna, you are never curious about anyone." He narrowed his eyes, "What's really going on?"

She looked at him and raised her eyebrow, to say, 'Like you don't know'.

"No!" he sarcastically gasped, "No way!"

"I can't stop thinking about him," she confessed, "I get butterflies in my stomach when I see him," she couldn't hold it back, "He was even in my dream—."

"What about the other guy?" Noah asked.

"He was there too, I'll tell you about the dream later," she leaned even closer to him, the other students were beginning to shuffle in, "What's worse," she began to whisper, "Is that Melina saw him first."

"So," Noah said annoyed, "That rule doesn't apply to you, and who cares, you saw him yesterday morning, before he walked into the school, remember?" He raised one eyebrow toward her,"You saw him first."

"You're right," Shayna knew that the rule didn't apply to her, and she felt ridiculous that she even cared. But *she* had seen him first.

"So what is your plan?" Noah asked grinning.

"I'm not sure yet," she told him, "I want to get to know him, and I'm going to tell Melina that I'm interested."

"Yeah?" he said, "You're going to tell her?"

"Well I should, and it should be sooner, rather than later," Shayna said, and then remembered why her and Noah had met early for in the first place. "What do you know about him?"

"He moved here from northern California with his aunt. I didn't ask him where his parents were, I figured he would have mentioned them, if they were around. But," he said, "They're going to turn that old place into a horse ranch."

"Really?" Shayna was intrigued, she absolutely loved horses. They were the only animal that didn't freak out around her. "That's good to know," she said. Since Shayna was fifteen she worked at a horse ranch near the Sleeping Bear Dunes during the summers. She was having a hard time accepting what she was, and wanted to get away from everything, and everyone, and it was the only thing she could get Sarah to agree to. Shayna stayed at the ranch during the week, and would come home on the weekends.

"What else do you know?" she asked Noah.

He smiled at Shayna, "He likes fine art," Noah knew that would get Shayna's attention. "And he likes drawing portraits of people."

"Wow," Shayna said, with a content smile, "This just keeps getting better."

Noah was amused. He had waited a long time for someone to catch Shayna's attention. He was starting to think it wouldn't happen. He wasn't sure if it was because Shayna had high standards in boys, or in herself...or both. She was too focused on her life, and meeting all of her expectations of herself, to care or worry about dating.

The teacher arrived to the classroom almost five minutes after the final bell rang. He began the class and Noah winked at Shayna and said, "Go girl!"

Shayna was on her way to lunch and Delany stopped her, "Hey Shay, where's Mel?"

"Cramps, is my guess," she said with a smile. They parted ways and Shayna decided to call and check on Melina. She wanted to make sure she was okay.

She headed for the nearest bathroom searching for her cell phone in her backpack. She ducked in and went to the farthest stall at the end, and locked the door. The students weren't allowed to use their phones while school was in session, but everyone broke the rules a little.

Melina's phone only rang. When the voicemail answered Shayna left her a message.

"Hey Mel," Shayna said into the phone, "It's me. You alive? Call me," she hung up, and put her phone back in her backpack.

She left the stall, opened the bathroom door, and stepped out right into Cain. He was able to grab both of her upper arms, and stop her before they collided. She felt the strength in his hands as he held her, she looked up at him. His grasp on her weakened when their eyes met.

"Sorry." She smiled and looked down embarassed. "I just keep running into people today."

"No harm done." His voice was music. He released her, and she could still feel his hands on her arms like electricity. "You seem like you are in a hurry," he said.

She *was* in a hurry. She had hoped to see *him* at lunch. But here he was, tall, dark, and handsome.

"Not really." She didn't know what else to say.

To be standing that close to her was almost unbearable to him. Everything about her was everything he had learned to crave and desire in the years that he had witnessed.

"I'm very sorry," he said quietly, "I have to go."

Without saying another word he turned and headed in the direction he had come from. Shayna stood in the hallway confused. What was that? she thought. Is he okay? She shook her head and turned in the direction of the cafeteria.

Cain left Shayna and went straight to his car. He climbed in, leaned the seat back and closed the door. He did not know how to control this new emotion that he was feeling. The only thing that he knew to do, was to run. He wanted her blood so bad, but didn't want to scar her soft ivory skin either. She was the most beautiful flower he had ever seen. Just to see her was hard. But to stand next to her, breath her in and feel his throat burn and ache for her, was something he had never felt before.

Will she be like the others? He wondered.

"No," he said out loud. Almost scaring himself. He refused to think of this girl like the others. This one is different, I won't let it happen. He closed his eyes and thought of her sweet innocent face. He vowed to himself that Shayna would not be like *them*. He knew what he had to do with her, and he knew that he would not be able to stay away from her in the meantime. He waited for three centuries to find her, and he wasn't about to just let her go. Not now.

He wondered if she was even aware of what she was, or how she had survived so long already without her father. He wasn't the the only one in the world that craved the blood that flowed through her veins. He got out of his flashy BMW and headed back into the school building. He realized walking in the doors, that Shayna was nestled in this small northern Michigan community for a reason. To be secluded. As far as Cain knew there was only one other being on the planet that knew about Shayna, and he was more of a threat to Cain, than her.

He went down the hall to the stairs and walked up. He tried to appear as much like the children of this learning instution, as he could. He approached a boy with sandy brown hair, and skin too tanned for winter. Instantly Shayna's face was in Cain's mind. The tan boy was thinking about her. The image in his mind changed from her face to her body. Cain became enraged when she stood before him, in his mind, in purple underwear. Cain passed the boy, and bumped into his shoulder, hard. The boy stumbled back, and they made eye contact.

"Watch it," Cain said to him, as serious, and as cold, as he could. His eyes burned into the boy's like fire.

The boy's eyes widened. He looked away fearfully, and headed down the stairs. Cain would have to watch this one. His mind works differently than most others. He thought.

Shayna walked into the art room, and was surprised and joyed to see Cain. Everyone was already positioned around the table. She had forgotten about the still life project. Shayna left her backpack at her table, took her sketchbook, and claimed her place. She looked over her shoulder, at Cain. He was intently looking down at his drawing. She watched him draw. He was perfect. He looked so beautiful and graceful sitting there. He looked up, and his emerald green eyes locked with hers. Although she was emarrassed that he had caught her looking at him, she couldn't look away from him. He held her gaze for a moment longer, and then looked back down, and continued drawing.

She couldn't believe the feeling that ran through her body when their eyes met. Magical, was the only word to describe it. Her emotions were going wild, but she liked the feeling. She tried not to look at him that often, because she was sitting right in his line of vision of the still life, and she didn't want him to think she was some kind of weirdo stalker. No wonder he is starring at me! She told herself. He has to try to see through me.

This was all very new to Shayna, especially the feeling she got in the pit of her stomach everytime their eyes met. She had never been this interested in a boy, and she didn't even know him. She continued with her own drawing, but her mind was preoccupied with thoughts of Cain, she even considered staying home from college to get the chance to know him better. Don't be an idiot! She told herself.

Shayna closed her locker and prepared herself for the walk home. Once outside, she scanned the student parking lot for Cain's car. It was nowhere in sight. She exited the campus thinking about the little book store she had seen. She decided to stop in. It opened today, she remembered.

It wasn't long before the little shop came into veiw. The open sign was made out of old redwood burrel. She opened the door and stepped in. It was a quant little place with incense burning, and numerous shelves, of what seemed like ancient books. Standing behind the counter was an older woman with white hair, that Shayna did not recognize. Shayna smiled sweetly, and gave her a 'Hello" and a nod.

"May I help you find anything Dear?" the woman asked her.

"No thank you," Shayna replied. "Not at the moment, anyway," Shayna ran her hand across a row of books. "I saw your sign, and thought I would browse around." Shayna was never much of a 'People Person', but this woman had a good vibe about her.

The woman stepped out from behind the counter. She wore a floor length floral skirt, and had a cane that looked like it was as ancient as the books in the store.

"Feel free to look around, I have some work to tend to in the back, but if you need anything, just holler, my assistant or I will be right with you." she told Shayna, with a very sweet smile.

Shayna didn't see an assistant, she had thought the two were alone in the store.

"Thank you" Shayna said, and returned the smile.

The frail woman walked slowly to the back of the store and disappeared around the corner. Shayna looked around the shop until she found the section she was looking for. She was a little surprised at the size of the selection.

MYTHS/LEGENDS/ and the PARANORMAL

She was hopeful that she would find something, anything. She knelt down to the floor, deciding to start at the bottom, and started scanning the titles. *Immortal Blood, Curse of the Night, and Sunlight.* She grabbed *Sunlight*, and kept scanning until she found one she thought might be helpful.

"No way," she whispered to herself. She reached for the book, her heart pounding, hoping it was what she thought it was. *The Halfling Princess* was the title. With the book in her hands she stood up, and took a step backwards.

"Whoa!" She heard, and, felt herself hit someone, knocking books onto the floor. "Sorry I didn't see you down there." Music.

Not again! She thought. Shayna was in shock. There stood Cain, more handsome than ever, holding a partial stack of books. He works here! She quickly put the two books that were in her hand behind her back.

Cain realized it was Shayna, and smiled and laughed, "I should have known it was you," he said, "I have never run into sombody, literally, so many times in one day, in my life."

"I'm sorry," she said, her cheeks flushed, "I really need to start watching where I'm going." She thought back to Derrick. "You're not the only one I've run into today," she told him, embarassed.

He laughed again, "Shayna, right?" He was trying to be coy.

"Right." She thought about the books she held in her hand, that she didn't want him to see. "Cain, right?" She liked his coyness.

"Are you finding everything okay?" he asked her, "This is definitely not your basic book store."

"I've noticed," she smiled at him, "It is very," she paused, "different. But yes, I am finding what I need,' she said and hoped. "I'm just about done."

Shayna dreaded what was coming next, he would have to see the books she was purchasing, and any hopes she had of getting to know him better would be gone. He would probably think she was a freak.

Cain looked toward the back, "Let me grab Aunt Mill for you, she'll be happy to help you."

Shayna couldn't believe her luck, although she was grateful at the moment, she didn't want him to go away either.

"She's your aunt?" She never would have guessed. There was no resemblance at all.

"Yes. We own the bookstore," he said, and looked toward the back again and whispered, "I know the store won't be hugely popular, but we're not trying to make money. We're trying to be informative. People don't know about this kind of stuff. Some want to know, while others deny it," he raised an eyebrow at Shayna, she was embarassed again.

She enjoyed talking with Cain, she had been waiting for this, but oh how she just wanted to pay for her books and hide them. She was disappointed when she realized he must have noticed her nervousness, and told her that Aunt Mill would be right out. He excused himself and walked to the back.

The old woman stepped out of the back and came to the counter. Up close Shayna could see that her old face looked oddly young, and beautiful. Her long silvery hair was pulled back in a loose braid, and it flowed down to her bottom. She must be his great aunt. Shayna thought to herself.

"Ahh." Her smiling face was comforting, "I'm glad you found something, dear."

"So am I," Shayna confessed, "Hopefully they're helpful."

This woman, Aunt Mill, picked up the books and read the titles, she quickly gave Shayna a suspicious look, and then smiled.

"I'm sure they will be, dear. I'm sure." The woman looked like joy had overcome her. Shayna was a little confused, "Please, come back and see me soon," she told Shayna, and handed her the change. Maybe she is just happy to have a customer. Shayna thought.

"I will," she said truthfully. And she would, especially if the two books did proved to be helpful. She put the books in her backpack and hoped Cain would come back out before she left. "Thank you," she said to Aunt Mill, and turned toward the door. Cain didn't return. She turned back to Aunt Mill, "Tell Cain I will see him tomorrow."

"Sure thing dear." The old woman's smile grew larger.

"Bye," Shayna said, and opened the door and walked out. She liked Aunt Mill. She thought she was very sweet, even if a little odd.

Cain watched Shayna leave from the back. He came out when she was out of sight, and walked to the counter.

"I can't believe she came in here," he said to Aunt Mill, who stood at the window watching Shayna walk down the road.

The woman looked at Cain with the same joy Shayna had seen, "She *is* magnificent Cain," she stated, "Did you see what she purchased?" she asked him.

"No," he recalled, and laughed, "She hid them behind her back as soon as she saw me. Huh, if she only knew."

"She knows, Cain," Aunt Mill couldn't stop smiling.

Cain looked at her trying to reach into her mind. "Knows what?" he finally asked.

The old woman narrowed her wrinkled eyes, "She knows what she is, and after she reads that book, she might just know what you are too," she answered him, and then said, "Not who you are, but what you are. If you really feel as strongly as you say you do about her, than you're are going to need to be honest with her. Don't hold back" she said.

Cain thought of Marcus Verona. He frowned. He didn't like the feeling of regret.

After leaving the book store, Shayna continued down Long Lake Road. She had wanted to stay and talk with Cain, but she also didn't want to push her luck. The book store had just opened, and she refused to let him think she was as desperate as the other girls at the academy.

She thought about the books in her backpack. She knew she had found what she needed. Her father had left her with very little information regarding her transformation. He had only told her what they both were, and that she was very special. He had also said that he would return for her, by her eighteenth birthday, and that only true death would stop him.

Shayna thought of Cain. She needed more of him, their encounters were too brief. She became frustrated. She turned onto Innwood, and something above caught her eye. The hawk was high above her, soaring in circles. Beautiful! she thought. She tried to ignore the creature when he seemed to be following her.

She thought of Cain again, and back to the bookstore. She remembered something she had seen on his hand. A ring with a very familiar looking gemstone in it. She couldn't believe that she hadn't realized it earlier. She had the same type of stone tucked away under a floorboard in her closet. It was dark green, with spots of red. It was there with the rest of her father's belongings that she had found in the attic, the day she decided to go snooping. She needed to find out what kind of gemstone it was. Her father had dozens of the stones, a ring and a beautiful necklace. The gemstone on the necklace had been faceted and cut into a large one and a half inch heart shape, with a small red tear drop carnelia, hanging from the bottom of the gemstone. It was accented by a pure silver chain, that Shayna was certain was at least five hundred years old. Give or take a couple hundred years. It was absolutely gorgeous.

Her attempts at ignoring the hawk worked. While she was deep in thought about this precious gemstone, the hawk disappeared. She approached her house, and walked in to find Melina laying on the couch with a heating pad on her abdomen.

"Ha! Just as I suspected." Shayna had never seen anyone miss so much school because of 'cramps'.

"Just wait Shayna," she smiled conivingly, "Yours is coming."

"Whatever," Shayna said, and wondered if she should tell her sister. Now or never. She decided. "Mel, I have to talk to you."

"What?" Melina said nervously, and then, "I didn't do it!"

"No," Shayna said, and sat down in a big over stuffed olive green chair, "You didn't do anything." She looked at Melina, "It's about me."

Melina sat straight up, "Ooh, I love gossip."

"Nevermind," Shayna said, ready to stand up and forget the whole thing.

"No Shay," Melina pleaded, "I'll be serious, don't go."

Shayna relaxed a little, "Okay, you have to think about what I'm saying before you respond."

Melina agreed, "Okay."

Twisting her hair, Shayna added, "And you can't tell anybody. Not yet anyway."

"Okay," she agreed again, "What it is?"

Shayna took a deep breath, "It's about the new boy Cain," she confessed. Melina raised her eyebrows, Shayna continued, "I think I am attracted to him." She stopped and waited for a response, she could see Melina process the information and grin.

"Go for it," she said, leaning back onto the couch again.

"What?" Shayna was surprised that it was that easy, "Really?"

"Well," she started, "Being home all day I realized that, I agree with Maria, he's out of our league." Melina looked at her twin with fascination, "But, if you like him, I say go for it." Melina was shocked at her sister's confession. "How did this happen?" she asked. Shayna seemed so dull and boring to Melina. But, if anybody can catch this boy's interest, it was Shayna. Melina thought.

"I don't know. I saw him yesterday, and he has been the center of my mind ever since. Even my dreams," Shayna was embarassed telling Melina this. She scratched at the chair with her finger. "I keep bumping into him too. Like, really bumping into him. I don't mean to, it's just happening," Shayna laughed in her head when she thought of it, but continued anyway, "The way I feel inside is making me crazy." She was talking without taking breaths in between now, "When I think about him, my knees get weak and my stomach flutters all over," she couldn't stop, "Is this normal? Am I okay? Wh—"

"Shay!" Melina interrupted her, "Calm down!" She sat up again. "Take a deep breath, you're fine," Melina laughed, "This is great."

"Please." Shayna used her eyes to plead with her sister, "Don't say a word. I want him to find out from me. Not through gossip." She thought of Cain, "He's too sophisticated for that."

Melina held out a hooked little finger to Shayna, "I pinky swear, I won't tell anyone." The girls locked pinky fingers and kissed their thumbs, to seal the deal.

"Thanks Melina."

"One question," Melina started, "Why did you tell me? You never tell me anything." She thought for a second, then said, "That kinda offends me, by the way."

"I told you because I thought you liked him, and I didn't want a problem." She lowered her eyes, Shayna hated confrontation, but believed being honest was more important, "At least I cared."

"Seriously Shayna," Melina was a little hurt, "I'm not shallow, and I do have a brain. Being clueless is just a role I like to play. I know when I'm in over my head, and I do care too." She smiled at her sister, leaned back, and readjusted the heating pad, "If you would have told me you liked him, I would have backed off. Nothing would make me happier than to see you finally hook up with somebody."

"Whatever." Shayna stood up, "We good then?" she asked.

"You bet." Melina picked the remote control up off the of coffee table, "Good luck. I think if anyone can catch his eye, it's you.

You're a dork," Shayna said, and walked out of the living room, hoping she had already caught his eye.

Shayna dropped her backpack on her bedroom floor, and went to her computer. She sat down at the desk, turned the computer on, and connected to the internet. On her Google bar she typed the words:
GEMSTONE GREEN STONE RED SPOTS

It was called a Bloodstone, her eyes widened, she clicked on the link to the Encyclopedia of Gems, and read the description.

Bloodstone is a dark green jasper stone that is dotted with iron oxide. The iron oxide resembling drops of blood. Also called Heliotrope, a greek word meaning sun and turning. A polished bloodstone was thought by ancients to reflect the sun. Bloodstone is said to be a very magical stone, it is said to strengthen blood purifying organs, and improve blood circulation.

Shayna shut down her computer, and leaned back in her chair. Sun and turning. She thought. She got up from the desk and locked the door. She looked around the room for her backpack, finding it on the bed. She sat on her bed and took the book *Sunlight* out of her backpack. She took in a deep breath and opened it.

Chapter 3

Shayna stepped into the meadow in awe of how captivating it was. She knew the meadow well. It was near the waterfall. The daisies were blooming, and the setting sun gave a purple glow behind the towering maple trees.

She looked down at herself, and gasped. She was dressed in a magnificent white gown, that was trimmed in silver, and sparkled in the dimming sunlight like diamonds. It flowed so beautifully to the ground, it reminded her of the waterfall. She knew it was from a different time period. A different era. A time Shayna only dreamed of.

She felt something touch her shoulder, and she spun around. She felt no fear. It's him. She wished she knew his name.

"My name is not important," he said, and took her hand.

Puzzled, she narrowed her eyes and said, "How did you do that?"

He smiled, his eyes like sapphires, and led her to a downed tree at the edge of the meadow, "I'm getting closer to you now, Shayna."

She was still confused, she sat down on the tree, and asked, "What do you mean?"

"Well," he said, "The closer I get to you, the stronger I am in your dreams. Your dreams tell me, that you want to know my name."

"I still don't understand," Shayna said, and picked up a daisy. The petals were like silk, and the center looked like gold glitter. So delicate.

"Let me exp—"

"Shayna. No!" someone was yelling on the other side of the meadow. Shayna looked past the boy, and saw Cain running toward them. He was getting closer. The boy turned quickly, and ran at Cain. In a rainbow of colors, he transformed into a hawk, a very large hawk, and was in the air soaring over Cain's head. Cain lunged at the hawk. He lunged high, but the hawk was gone.

Shayna stared in awe, speechless. She couldn't believe how high Cain had jumped. He hit the ground hard but gracefully, and walked toward her.

"I told you that I'm here for you now," he said as he approached her, "But, I'm not the only one."

She didn't know whether to be scared, or inquisitive.

"Who is he?" she asked and reached for his hand, she felt comfortable doing it, it felt right to her. "Is he real?"

He took her hand and looked into her eyes. Her knees weakened, and gave out. He caught her in his arms, and lifted her up, their eyes still locked.

"I'm real," he said.

"Shayna, what are you doing in there?" The doorknob on Shayna's door rattled, "Open up," Melina was calling to Shayna from the other side.

Shayna sat up, the room was dark. She looked at the clock on her nightstand, and turned on the lamp. It was 6:33pm.

"Shay," Melina said again.

"Hold on, I was sleeping." Shayna found her books on the bed, stuffed them into her backpack, and got up and opened the door.

"Noah called," Melina said, as soon as the door was open, "He said he called your phone but you didn't answer," she stood on her tiptoes trying to peek into the room, "What are you doing?"

"I told you, I was sleeping," Shayna answered, "What are *you* doing, faker?"

"I'm not faking," Melina said, with a smirk, "I'm better now."

"Whatever." Shayna was getting impatient, "Did Noah say what he wanted?"

"No, he just said to have you call him," Melina said, and turned to head down the stairs, "I'm warming up last nights spaghetti, if you're hungry," she added, over her shoulder.

Shayna waited until she could hear Melina was downstairs, then closed and locked her door again. She got the books out of her backpack, and found a flat head screwdriver in her desk, and went to her closet. She knelt down to the right corner and pried up the floorboard. She placed the books in the small space in the closet floor. She pulled a shoebox out of the space, opened it, and brought out a silver box that was inside. She removed a velvet pouch from the silver box, replaced the board and went back to her bed. She held the velvet pouch tight in her hand and closed her eyes.

Shayna woke up the next morning to Melina jumping on her bed.

"Shay, wake up," she said with excitement. "Look outside."

"Come on," Shayna said, and tried to roll Melina off of her. "Get off of me!"

Melina removed herself from her sister, jumped off the bed, and opened the dark purple sun and moon patterned drapes, that were concealing the day.

"Look."

Shayna sat up and peered out the window.

Everything was white. Her eyes widened, and her jaw dropped in a sarcastic way.

"Is that snow?" she asked.

"Can you believe it?" Melina had a grin from ear to ear. She loved snow days, and missing school, but she didn't like the cold. "I was starting to think that it wasn't ever going to snow this year."

Shayna got out of bed and went to the window. The hardwood floor of her bedroom was cold on her bare feet. She looked out. Everything was covered, it wasn't just a light dusting that the weathermen had called for. There was a thick blanket over everything, and it was still coming down.

"It's so beautiful," Shayna whispered, "And silent." She peered out the window and watched the snow fall.

"There's no school," Melina told her interrupting Shayna's moment, "Apparently everyone forgot how to drive in this stuff. Idiots."

Shayna shot a look of disappointment at Melina, "What? We have to miss school for *this*?" She really didn't mind missing school, but she was missing Cain.

"Don't worry Miss Perfect," Melina said to her, rolling her eyes, "Your perfect attendance record won't be shattered. You can make it up at the end of the year." With a smirk, Melina walked out of the room.

Shayna didn't care if Melina thought her attendance record was the reason she didn't want to miss school. She really didn't want Melina to know how strongly

she was feeling for Cain. She had already told Melina
too much. Now that she knew why he would wear a
bloodstone ring, she *really* didn't want Melina to know
too much. She sighed. She wanted to see Cain, she
needed to see him.

She put on a plush pink robe, and went downstairs.
Melina was on the phone, probably with Maria or
Delany, on the couch. Shayna went to the big picture
window in the living room, and looked out at the
neighborhood. She didn't want to be cooped up all day.
She wasn't going to let a couple inches of snow keep
her inside. She went to the kitchen and had a bowl of
cereal, and a bagel. Then went upstairs to take a bath
and decide what to do with the snow day.

When she was out of the bath she went back to her
room. She dug through her closet, wrapped in a towel,
for the warmest clothes she could find. Buried way in
the back, she found a box she hadn't seen in two years.
Her grandmother had sent it to her. Somehow it had
gotten shoved to the back of her closet, to be forgotten
about. She grabbed the box and a pair of jeans, and sat
down on the bed with them.

"Perfect," she said to herself.

Inside was a pair of brown, almost knee high, leather
lace up boots that were lined with thick fur and wool,
and a matching hooded coat. I can't believe I forgot
about these. She thought.

Once dressed she looked in the mirror. She looked
like an eskimo princess, like she was dressed for a
frozen tundra. The coat hugged her body, and hung just
over her buttocks. Along with the thermal pants she
wore under her clothes, and the two pairs of socks she
had on, she knew she would be plenty warm enough.

She went downstairs to the kitchen and found a
water bottle, and filled it. Melina was still veged out on

the couch when Shayna came into the living room to talk to her.

"I'm going for a walk to the meadow," she told Melina, "I'll be back in a couple of hours."

"You're crazy," Melina said, and looked at her sister. "Look at *you!*" she exclaimed, "You look hot. Are you meeting *Cain* in the meadow?"

Shayna glared at Melina, "I'm going for a walk." Although, she did wish she was meeting Cain in the meadow, "Can't I be warm and look good too?"

"Well have fun," Melina looked outside and frowned, "I'm going to stay right here," she said pointing to the couch.

"See ya, then," Shayna said, and whirled around on her heels, and went through the kitchen and out the backdoor. Grabbing a pair of gloves out of the seat of the bench as she passed.

The cold air hit her face hard, almost taking her breath away. She pulled the hood of the coat over her head, the fur lining doing a good job of keeping snow flakes out of her face. She hugged herself and shivered.

"What am I doing?" she said, under her breath.

She put on the gloves, and stepped off the porch. She carried the water bottle by it's strap and,headed in the direction of the path, which had disappeared under the snow. Even though she couldn't see it, she knew where it was.

She used the trees that she knew very well, to guide her way through, and it payed off. She arrived at the waterfall about forty five minutes later. She followed the path past, thinking she should have brought her sketch book with her. The way the weather had been lately, who knew when it would snow again. She trudged through the snow in the direction of the meadow for another hour before she finally stepped into the clearing. She had come because of something she had seen in her dream. Something that wasn't what she remembered of the meadow. The fallen tree. She knew there wasn't a tree down the last time she had been there. But she also knew to pay attention to her dreams.

There it was. Her widened eyes focused on the tree. She walked across the meadow toward it. She hadn't been here since the summer, and wondered how long it had been down for. The roots had came up out of the ground when the tree fell. It was an older maple, but appeared dwarfed to Shayna. She was almost to it when she heard a crunch in the snow, and saw movement in the trees at the edge of the meadow. Suddenly, in a blur, there was Cain. He stood in front of her looking determined. He had the most serious look on his face. It frightened Shayna.

"Don't move Shayna," his eyes were wide, "He's dangerous and unpredictable."

Shayna was terrified. She froze. A million things flashed through her mind. Horrible things, bloody things. She had read enough the night before to know what they were capable of. Her eyes were focused on Cain, his eyes were full of…fear. In the moment she realized that he was trying to help her, she felt a push in the middle of her back. Shayna gasped, she tried to scream, but nothing came out. Her throat was too dry from the cold air.

"Shayna," Cain said, and stepped toward her with his hands held up defensively.

She turned slowly. She knew she wasn't dreaming, but she wished she was. She didn't want to see what or who was behind her.

A huge black figure loomed over her, and she was blinded by the white of the snow, and the sun peeking through the clouds. Shayna had to blink until her eyes focused. She was in awe.

"Please don't move too suddenly?" Cain begged.

She heard crunching snow behind her. Cain was closing in.

Shayna smiled, and the massive beast stepped toward her. She put her hand out, palm up and it placed it's huge wet, velvety muzzle in her cupped hand. With her other hand she reached up to his head and scratched between his ears.

"He's amazing," she said to Cain when he stood next to her. "Is he a Friesian?"

"He is," he looked at Shayna in disbelief. "How do you know?"

"I work at a horse ranch in the summer. This is my favorite breed," Shayna put her hand under his forelock and rubbed his head there. The huge black horse pushed his head into Shayna's little body in delight, and she stumbled into Cain's arms, "He likes that," she said, laughing and regaining her footing in the snow..

"This is amazing," Cain said. He was in awe too, "This horse is the most dangerous horse I have ever owned, or encountered. Yet he is like a kitten in your hands."

She smiled at him, She couldn't decide who was more beautiful, Cain or the horse. He looked so handsome standing there in the snow, he wore no coat or jacket. Just a light blue, cotton button up shirt, and a pair of khaki slacks. It seemed so odd to Shayna.

"What are you two doing here?"

Cain pointed toward the horse, "He likes to take me on adventures," he said smiling, "He's an escape artist."

Shayna examined the horse. He was very tall, at least seventeen hands, and jet black. His mane flowed down past his neck, and his tail trailed on the ground behind him. He's perfect. She thought.

"What is his name?" she asked Cain.

"Obsidion," he replied, then changed the subject, "Ya know, he was following you for a while. Don't you ever look around you? You should be more observant out here by yourself."

"I grew up in these woods," she told him. "If there was anything dangerous out here, I would know."

"What about him?" Cain said, pointing at Obsidion, but thinking of himself. "I've seen him kill two of my stable hands, and break a trainer's back, and *I* had to tell you he was behind you. You didn't have the slightest glimmer of danger in your thoughts." Cain knew that *he* was more of a danger to her, than his horse.

"He's not dangerous," she rubbed her hands down the horses neck and over his back, as far up as she could reach. Obsidion stomped his right front hoof into the snow, with a thud, and grunted.

"He's not dangerous to *you* apparently," Cain said, in observation. "I've never seen anything like it, it's like he's known you forever."

Shayna was mesmerized by the creature. Cain reached for his halter and Obsidion rared up , and pulled away from him.

"Whoa!" he said putting his hands up.

When the horse was on all fours again Shayna reached for his halter, and grabbed it with a firm grip pulling him towards her. He calmed instantly, and stood next to her. His hot breath visible in the cold air when he snorted.

"Easy," Shayna whispered to him. He snorted again. She looked at Cain, "You make him nervous."

"He makes me nervous!" he said, with a chuckle, "Will you help me get him back?"

How could she say no, to those eyes. Those eyes that were *not* shy?

"How?" she asked.

"Maybe he'll follow you," Cain said hopeful, "He followed you this far."

Shayna gestured for Cain to go, "Lead the way," she told him. He turned and started to walk by the tree. She followed but Obsidion did not. "This isn't working."

"Come on Sid," Cain pled in frustration, and turned around. The horse stomped the ground and whinnied, and Shayna laughed.

"Is he rideable?" she asked him.

Cain returned to her side. "He used to be, but nobody has been able to get on his back in two, maybe, three years," he looked down at her, she was starring at the horse.

"Can I try?" she asked, turning her eyes up to Cain.

"I don't know," he said, and stomped at the ground like Obsidion had, "I would feel horrible if something happened to you."

Before he could say anything else, Shayna was walking toward the horse.

"Wait!" he called after her.

"Just give me a leg up," she said.

She stood beside Obsidion, and Cain rushed to her side. He wasn't used to taking orders, but it felt right to obey when Shayna was the one giving them.

She gathered Obsidions mane above his withers, and Cain lifted her up by her leg until she was able to finally pull the other leg over the horse's back. Obsidion stood perfectly sill through the process, and hoofed the ground again, once Shayna was sitting atop of him. Cain looked at Shayna and the horse. She was so petite and Obsidion was so massive, Bella Vista. He thought to himself. Shayna was focused on the horse. She squeezed her heels into his side, and was pleased when he began to step forward.

Cain watched in amazement as they walked past him. His old obsession, and his knew one. They talked about Obsidion while they walked, and about how Cain had acquired him. He told her a story of how he saved the horse from a trainer who would have killed him, if Cain hadn't been walking through the stable at a horse show, and found them. He had bought Obsidion for quite a substantial amount of money. But Cain was starting to think the horse was crazy.

Shayna had other things on her mind. She had questions she wanted to ask him. She looked down at him walking next to horse. She saw his ring. She knew why he wore it. Underneath her clothes she wore her fathers necklace. She had taken it out of it's velvet sanctuary and put it on before she went to bed.

She swallowed hard, "Do you know what I am?" she asked him. This stopped Cain in his tracks. "Whoa!" she said to Obsidion. The horse stopped abruptly. She faced Cain. She had caught him off guard.

He slowly looked up at Shayna. His emerald green eyes sparkled in the snow, and his hair fell around his face, almost framing it. He was beautiful, if a guy could be.

He nodded his head, "Yes, I do," he said and remained motionless.

"Am I really," Shayna thought for a moment to find the right words, "What is called a Halfling Princess?"

Cain returned to their side and looked up at Shayna, "Yes," he said.

She felt dizzy, looking down at him, but continued, "So, when I turn eighteen, I will stop aging, and I will no longer be mortal?"

Cain reached up and squeezed her gloved hand, "That's correct."

Shayna's expression turned to worry, "Will it hurt?" she asked Cain.

"It shouldn't," Cain said with sympathy in his eyes, "But every princess is different, I guess, and you are one of a kind. So I don't know for sure. I'm sorry."

"How long does it take?" Shayna squeezed her legs around Obsidion's belly and he walked forward.

Cain strolled beside them, and said, "I don't know how long it takes." He looked at the ground while they walked. "I've never witnessed the change."

"And the bloodstone will protect me from the sun, when I change?" Shayna was full of questions. She never had anyone to ask them to before. She wanted to ask the right ones.

"Yes, but you have to wear it outside of your clothes." He pointed to the silver chain around her neck.

"Do I need it now?" she asked, reaching into her sweater to pull the gemstone out.

"No, I guess not." His eyes caught her bloodstone, "Where did you get *that*?" he said, with great interest.

"It was my fathers," she responded, holding the necklace in her hand, she looked at it. "Why?"

"These stones aren't that easy to come by, for the most part, and they need to be polished to be effective." He pointed at Shayna's necklace, "But, *that* is very rare. Do you not see the flecks of platinum in it?"

Shayna held the stone in her hand, and rubbed the smooth surface. It did look different from the pictures on the internet. She thought.

They were finally approaching his place. She could see Aunt Mill through an upstairs window watching them walk into the barn. It wasn't long after they had Obsidion in his stall, with a blanket, oats, and hay, when Aunt Mill showed up with a single cup of steaming hot cocoa.

"You must be frozen dear," she said to Shayna, handing her a silver mug.

"Mmm, thank you," Shayna said, and took the mug. "Sid kept me warm for the most part." She took a sip of the cocoa.

"If you two need anything else, just let me know." She smiled at Cain and Shayna, and turned and walked out of the barn.

"Thank you, we will," Cain told the sweet old lady before she disappeared out of sight. He looked at Shayna and asked, "Can I tell you anything else Princess?"

She smiled. He awoke something deep inside of her when he called her Princess.

"How old are you?" she asked, and stepped closer to him.

"More than three hundred years old," he answered her.

She was face to face with him, "What is going to happen to me?" Shayna was glad to have someone she could talk to, and oddly enough, she felt like she had known Cain all her life.

"You're going to be fine," he said, trying not to make it sound like a lie. He didn't want it to be a lie, he hoped it wasn't. "You will have to drink blood to survive. Not just one or twice a week, like you have been."

"Which is why my mom brings the blood home from the hospital, she keeps in the basement freezer?" she asked him.

"Yes," he said, "Does your mom know?"

Shayna mindlessly played with the buttons on Cains shirt and said, "The letter I found from my father, said she didn't. But he had told her how important it was for her to keep her job at the hospital and always make sure I hade some source of blood at least once a week." Shayna had never told anyone about the letter, or what it read, and it sounded bizzare hearing herself say it out loud. She frowned.

"What else did your father's letter say?" Cain inquired.

She took a deep breath and let it out loudly, "He said, he would be back for me, by the time I turned eighteen. He had faked his death, because he had been in northern Michigan for too long, and people were starting to notice that he wasn't aging. He wanted me to stay here, with my family, but that was before my grandparents moved to Canada. He said if he *didn't* come back, that it would be because he was really dead."

Cain frowned himself, and looked to the ground at her feet, "I'm sorry."

"I'm starting to think he isn't coming back." A tear fell on to her cheek, "My birthday is in just a couple weeks."

Cain saw the tear and placed his hand on the side of her neck, and wiped it away with his thumb. His hand was ice on her skin.

"I'm here for you now," he said looking deep into her eyes. Shayna was in her own *Utopia* with Cain. "I'll help you through this, you won't have to do it alone."

She was lost in his eyes and speechless. The way he looked at her made her think he was going to kiss her.

She was disappointed when he didn't. He moved his hand away from her and stepped back.

"I should probably get you home," he said.

Shayna didn't want to leave, she wanted him to hold her, to tell her everything would be okay.

She went to Obsidion's stall to say goodbye to the massive horse. She walked out of the barn, and could hear him kicking his stall. They got to Cain's car and he walked to the passenger side and opened the door for her. She sat down on the black leather seat, and inhaled the car's air. She loved the smell of new leather in a car. The seats in the BMW were cold, but they warmed up fast, once the car was running. He drove a lot slower than what Shayna had witnessed at the school.

"Do you kill people?" she asked him. Again catching him off guard. He didn't like that she was able to do it, but it was part of her mystique.

"I have," he said, after a while. "I don't anymore, that's what I have the horse's for, their blood is almost as strong, it doesn't taste nearly as satisfying, but it works."

Shayna looked at Cain in disgust, "What about Obsidion?"

"Not him. And I value my horses. I don't take all of their blood." He shot a look in Shayna's direction. She didn't like the sound of what he was saying. "He's a lot like you. I have to be able to impel his mind, so I don't hurt him or myself, and I can't. I get nothing." Cain smiled at the thought of his horse. "I've never seen anything like the two of you."

"What do you mean *impel*?" Shayna asked. Her stomach twisting at the thought of the horses.

"It's kind of like mind control, I guess," Cain admitted, "I impel them into a trance, to calm their minds. That way they don't get hurt, and they don't remember what happened either."

"Can you do it to humans?" Shayna asked him.

"With the exception of one." He looked at her with a raised eyebrow.

"Me?"

"I can't read your thoughts, I can't feel your emotions, I can't impel you. Nothing," he paused then said, "It's kind of frustrating."

"Why would you want to impel *me*?" she asked and glared at him.

Cain was quick to answer, "I don't, I'm just saying that even *if* I wanted to, I couldn't. I don't know what it is about you Shayna, but you're different than any other being that I have ever encountered.

He licked his lips, hoping she did not see his extended canines. His mouth watered for her. The scent of her blood filled his car, and burned his throat.

"I can't keep myself away from you," he confessed, "For the last few weeks all I could think about was how to get close to you. And now you're sitting in my car, and I don't have any inkling to what is on your mind. And your blood," he breathed her in deep, and Shayna thought she saw a flash of red is his green eyes, "Your blood is so overpowering."

Shayna didn't know what to say to him. They turned on to her street, and she realized that not once, had she told him where to go. She was more intrigued.

"You've known about me?" she said.

"For a while," Shayna started to say something, but Cain interrupted her, "Shayna, I am dangerous to you," he said, and accelerated the BMW toward her house, "I crave your blood, your human blood. Do you understand that?"

Shayna looked out the window and silently nodded her head.

They pulled up to her house and she finally asked, "Do you want to hurt me?"

"No," he said. "God no. I don't think I could ever forgive myself if I ever hurt you."

She reached across the car and took his hand, it was so cold. She wondered if she would be the same way.

"Trust yourself," she told him, "I trust you. You could have taken my blood in the woods today. You're not going to hurt me." She held his hand tight, not wanting to let go.

"You are absolutely amazing." He smiled and moved a strand of hair away from her eyes. "You're so vulnarable right now, and you don't even care."

"Not in the slightest."

She couldn't move. Cain was so enticing. She was once again lost in his eyes. She wanted to be his princess, and she one hundred percent believed, deep in her heart, that he would never hurt her physically, emotionally, or spiritually.

She touched his hair. It was soft and hung just below his chin. He leaned his face into her hand. She wanted him. She yearned for him. He was right, she didn't care if he thought he was a danger to her. She knew he wasn't. Their secrets had drawn them to each other.

They sat in front of her house for about twenty minutes, talking and making plans to go horseback riding. The emotions flooding through her body were indescribable. Her heart was pounding, and she felt like she was going to hyperventilate.

"Where are we going?" she asked, about their ride.

"It's a secret," he smiled.

"I've lived here all my life. I know where everything is," she said, with a smirk, "So go ahead and keep your secret."

"That's fine if you do know. I still want to take you there," Cain said, and gestured past Shayna toward the house, "We have an audience."

Shayna looked over her shoulder, and saw Melina peeking through the closed curtains of the big front window. She turned back to Cain.

"What time shall I be there?" she asked him, fluttering her long dark eye lashes at him.

He laughed at this, "Around nine," he said, still chuckling. He took her hand and kissed it, "Farewell my Princess. Until Saturday we part."

Shayna felt her cheeks burn, "Bye," she was able to say, but it was barely a whisper.

She climbed out of the car, and closed the door. She stood on the curb and he slowly pulled away, accelerating the BMW faster, a couple houses down from Shayna's. She made her way up the walkway, and to the front door. Melina never missed a beat when Shayna opened the door.

"What is *that*?" she asked Shayna, before the door was even closed.

"What?"

"You said you weren't meeting anyone,"she reminded Shayna, "And five hours later, you come home with *him*!"

Shayna smiled, her eyes sparkled, and she said, "Funniest thing," she took her boots and coat off, and sat down on the couch, "I walked into the meadow and he was there, with a horse. The horse had gotten loose and lead him there. I helped him get him back to his house." She pulled the blanket off of the back of the couch and tucked it around herself.

"Uh-huh," Melina said suspiciously, "You move fast don't you?"

"Shut up Mel," she said, annoyed, "I'm not kidding. We have a real connection, and a lot in common," Shayna couldn't believe what she was sayin. Is this even real? She wondered.

"What, you're *both* beautiful and boring?" Melina said.

"Pretty much," Shayna agreed spitefully.

She knew that her and Cain were anything but boring. They made Melina look boring. Although Shayna had always thought that predicatable Melina was a bit boring, anyway. Shayna lay down onto a big couch pillow, and pulled the blanket over her.

"Cold?" Melina asked. "I told you that you were crazy for going out there."

Shayna closed her eyes, and thought of Cain, "I would do it again in a heart beat," she said, getting cozy deeper into the couch.

"I bet you would," Melina had a hunch about how her twin truly was feeling about this boy. She had always wanted to feel it herself. A car horn sounded outside. "Maria's here, we're going to grab a bite, do you want to go?" Shayna didn't answer, "Shay?"

Melina walked over to the couch and looked at Shayna who was completely unconscious, and snoring a little. Melina smiled and tucked the blanket around her sleeping twin, more. She wanted details but they would have to wait. Instead, she left with her friend.

Chapter 4

Cain walked out of the stall leaving the Quarter horse mare lying in the hay, with labored, but stable, breathing. He found a rag laying on a saddle, and used it to wipe his face. He left the barn and walked into the house to find Aunt Mill, cooking goulash on the stove. She had been with Cain for a few years. He had found her wandering in an alley in Eureka California. She had been babbling something about the "One", "The One that would save him." He couldn't seem to get rid of her, and beside the fact that he thought she was a witch of some sort, she turned out to be a very intellegent, wonderful old woman, and he had soon come to adore her. She knew what he was from the start, and it never seemed to bother her. She had been the one, who insisted Cain come to Michigan.

"Long day dear?" she asked, when he sat down. She could tell by his eyes that he had just fed. The red ring around his pupil still remained, and gave it away.

He looked at the aging woman, frail, and old, "How am I going to do this?" he asked her.

She sat down across from him, at the table.

"Cain dear," her eyes looked tired, and full of concern, "Maybe you should just stay away from her for a while. At least until she is eighteen. Then you won't have to worry about being a danger to her," she suggested.

"I wish I could," he said, and looked out the window, "But I can't. I ache without her. I need her near me physically. As much as I want to stay away from her, and keep her safe, I can't."

The pot on the stove started bubbling over, and Aunt Mill rushed to tend to it.

"I hate myself for putting her in danger like this," Cain said, and hit the table hard with his fist.

"Then why do it, child?" Aunt Mill said, stirring oregano into the pot.

Cain loved the smells of the food she cooked. He would never eat it, but it smelled delicious.

"I try," he scratched his head in frustration, something he had done since childhood, "She keeps showing up where ever I go. Who would have thought that damn horse would find her out there in the woods, in the middle of a mini blizzard? I was tracking him all night, and then there she was."

"That is a little ironic," Aunt Mill said, and then paused and smiled, "A little poetic too."

Cain, lost in his thoughts, finally said, "I've been able to control myself so far," he thought of Shayna's beautiful face, "As long as I never taste her mortal blood, I think I might be okay."

"Hopefully." She raised an eyebrow at him from the stove. Then suddenly she shook her head, dismissing the thought that he would hurt Shayna, "You know what dear? Your're right. You'll do just fine, trust yourself," she told him.

"She told me the same thing," he remembered, "To trust myself."

"She seems like a smart, inquisitive girl," Aunt Mill said, "You're very lucky Cain."

"He's here, you know?" Cain told her, changing the subject completely.

Aunt Mill looked at Cain, with wide eyes, "Will he hurt her?" she asked.

"No." He answered, "Thank God. But, he will be a nuisance, I'm sure, and try to keep us away from each other. Oh, and he might try to kill me." He smiled at her, "But, he's not after her. He's here to protect her."

"From you?" Aunt Mill asked him.

He knew what she was getting at, "I can't just walk away from her, and leave her alone."

"I know Cain." Everything was beginning to become clear to the old woman, "If you leave her, it will crush her, it will kill her spirit. You have to stay and see this thing through. She needs you," she said and paused, "You need her."

Cain looked up at her. He knew she spoke only words of wisdom and knowledge, and that deep inside, she knew something that he did not.

I need her. After hundreds of years, Cain never thought he would need anyone. He liked the sound of needing Shayna.

"You need each other," Aunt Mill said.

Cain noticed her look out the window in a peculiar way. He got up and stood behind the old woman, and looked out himself. The sun was setting, but the two of them could see the dark silhouette of a large bird perched on the roof of the barn.

A growl erupted from deep inside Cain's throat, and Aunt Mill gasped. Cain turned and ran out the back door. Aunt Mill saw him run through the snow covered yard toward the barn, and the hawk flew down towards him. Then she saw the Panther. She couldn't believe it. She had heard of this creature, but had never seen it herself. It was incredible. He was all black, with white around his neck, that looked like a collar, and white paws. He looked like he wore a tuxedo.

The panther leapt at the hawk, caught a mouthful of tail feathers, and ripped them out. The unusually large bird let out a defining screech, and clawed at the panthers face then took off over the barn, and out of sight.

Aunt Mill stared from the window in fascination. She could not peel her eyes away from the grizzly bear sized panther standing in her yard. They both knew that the hawk was no match for him. The panther turned and looked at her. In the fading daylight, she saw bright emerald green eyes, ringed in red. She nodded her head in acceptance, and the panther roared. The sound rumbled in her chest, she smiled. She had never witnessed anything like this in her life, and she had witnessed *a lot.*

Shayna opened her eyes, thinking she had heard thunder. She thought she was still dreaming for a second. She looked around the room, she was still on the couch. What weird weather. She thought. She tried to remember back to the dream she was having. The meadow had become a battlefield. She sat upon Obsidion's back beside the newly downed tree, and watched the hawk she had seen, and an enormous panther, fight over a blood red rose. They looked as though they would fight to the death, when the hawk suddenly flew away taking the rose with it. It had definitely been one of the weirdest dreams she had ever had.

She sat up on the couch, Was that thunder? It was part of the dream, I bet.She thought. She looked outside, it was snowing again. A couple of kids had built a snowman across the street, that she could see under the streetlight. She thought of the long life that was ahead of her, and of drinking blood. She knew that once she changed, the small amounts her mother gave her would never be enough, and she would have to drink more.

"How am I going to do this?" she asked herself. She was scared. In a couple weeks, she would be thrown into a world that most people didn't know existed, or even believed existed.

Her phone rang upstairs. She jumped up, and ran upstairs to get it, but was too late, she had missed the call. It was Noah. She put the phone back down on her dresser. She decided she would talk to him at school. She sat down on the bed and thought of her father. She wondered how he had hid their secret from her mother. Didn't she ever ask why? She wondered.

When her stomach growled, she realized she had not eaten all day, and she went down stairs. Smiling to herself along the way. The hairs on the back of her neck stood up, when she thought of Cain's face. She had enjoyed the time they were able to spend together, and couldn't wait to see him again.

Chapter 5

The snow had stopped, and was mostly gone by Friday morning. School remained cancelled, since they had missed most the week already. Shayna had spent most of Thursday shopping with Melina and Sarah in Traverse City. Melina needed a dress for the Winter Formal, and Shayna needed new boots. It drove her crazy that she hadn't been able to see Cain. She had gone to bed early, in hopes that he would visit her, in her dreams, but she had been disappointed. She remained in bed most of the morning listening to The Rock Station, and reading Utopia, and finally decided to go to 'Between the Lines.'

She hoped Cain would be there, but was going to see about finding another book, or two. Melina had taken their car and she was forced to walk. She scanned the trees for the hawk she had seen, wondering if it had any connection to the one in her dream, but it was nowhere in sight.

She walked into the book store, and was immediately greeted with the smell of incense, and a calming feeling. Aunt Mill was putting books on a shelf that was labled 'Philosophy', and when she saw Shayna, her face lit up with excitement.

"Shayna dear," she said, with an inviting smile. She put the last book on the shelf, and she turned to Shayna, "I'm so glad to see you again."

"I like your store," Shayna told her looking around, "It's very, inviting."

"Is there anything I can help you with today?" Aunt Mill asked.

Shayna could see stacks of books on the counter, and didn't want to keep her too long.

"Well," Shayna hesitated. Should I? She asked herself. She lowered her voice, she didn't know if Cain was in the store or not, "In one of the books I bought, it said something about Changeling vampires. Do you have anything on them?"

"Well," the old woman said, and blinked. Shayna saw something change in her eyes, just a twinge of something. She wasn't sure what it was. "There isn't a whole lot of written material on Changelings dear. Like you, they are rare creatures."

"Do *you,* know anything about them?" Shayna asked, hopeful that she would.

Aunt Mill stared at Shayna for a moment, then sighed and said, "I do know a little. What can I tell you?"

Shayna laughed a little, "I'm not sure. Anything you can, I guess."

"Do you know what a Changeling is?" she asked Shayna.

"No," Shayna answered, looking towards the back of the store where Cain might be.

Aunt Mill noticed, "He's not here today, dear," she told her.

Shayna was disappointed. She twisted her hair nervously, she wondered what she was doing. "Up until two years ago, I didn't even know what I was," she told the woman, assuming Aunt Mill knew too.

"Changelings are vampires, that are ususally created carelessly, or by mistake. Very rarely does it start off intentional." She looked at Shayna with eyes filled with care, and knowledge.

This was all becoming more confusing to Shayna, "By mistake?" she asked.

"Yes dear. If a vampire is changing a human, and it doesn't take enough of the humans blood, before the human takes the vampires in return, the human will either not change and possibly die, or, it will become a changeling, and will not have the powers and abilities, that a full vampire would have." Aunt Mill switched her cane to her other hand, and shifted her weight onto the same side.

"Do you need to sit down?" Shayna asked her, and looked around, to no avail, for the chair that was usually by the register.

"No dear, I'm fine," the woman insisted. She smiled at Shayna and continued, "Another way a Changeling is created, is for a vampire to drain the human of most of their blood, and then the human consumes a *different* vampires blood," Shayna was fascinated, she stared at Aunt Mill in awe, as she went on, "This usually doesn't happen child. The most common reason this particular act happens, is when the human is left for dead by a careless vampire, and another vampire finds him, and acts as a savior. The original vampire intended on killing the human."

Shayna thought about taking blood from a human, and her stomach churned. Images and questions ran through Shayna's mind, and she stared at Aunt Mill while she spoke.

"Vampires these days are more careful, and as a result there aren't very many Changelings anymore. They've either changed, or died. They are more prone to death."

"Changed?" Shayna said quietly.

"Yes dear. Changed to a full vampire, with no mortal blood in their body." Aunt Mill replied. She wondered if she was telling Shayna too much.

"How?" Shayna asked, perplexed. "How do they change?"

Aunt Mill took a deep breath, and closed her eyes briefly. Shayna thought she saw a look of remorse when she opened them, but in a blink it was gone.

Aunt Mill took Shayna's hand. "You dear," she said.

"Me?" Shayna was confused. What did she have to do with their change. She wondered.

"Yes dear." She squeezed Shayna's hand gently, Shayna noticed her hands were unusually soft, and dry. "They need *your* blood to change. The blood of a Halfling Princess. It must take place the last night that the girl is seventeen, and the two must intimately exchange blood, to consummate the arrangement."

Shayna was intrigued by what she was being told, but terrified too. There were so many things about this world she would probably never understand. She wanted to know as much as she could though, and Aunt Mill for the time was willing to talk to her.

Aunt Mill continued, "There are a few rare accounts of a Changeling, changing without ever tasting a princesses blood." She shook her head at this, and watched a young boy walk his dog past the shop, "Nobody knows how they changed though."

"No body at all?" Shayna asked.

"No dear. You Halfling Princesses are rare yourselves, so a Changelings odds of ever changing, are not that good anyway." She knew Shayna was uninformed on the subject, and the old woman had much sympathy for her. "Vampires usually don't breed with humans," she said, and picked up a stack of books off the counter, "Can I help you with anything else dear?"

Shayna did want more help, but knew Aunt Mill was probably busy.

"No," she answered. "I think you've helped me enough today, thank you."

"Anytime, Shayna dear," Aunt Mill said and nodded. "Hope to see you again soon."

"You will," Shayna said, and turned toward the door, "Bye."

She left the little shop, more informed, but disappointed too. She had hoped to find a book that she could read herself, so she could absorb as much information as possible. What Aunt Mill had told her was more than she thought she would find, but she regretted not asking more questions. Although she didn't know what questions to even ask. Of course once outside the store, she thought of tons of questions she should have asked. She had one more stop to make, before heading home. She crossed the street and turned onto Railroad Avenue.

Shayna walked through the gates of the cemetary and, was stricken with an unusual feeling. More unusual than the cemetary normally felt. Eerie. She thought. She walked down the first aisle of headstones, and made a right towards her fathers memorial. She felt alone in the world, as she made her way through the cemetary by herself.

She hated coming to the cemetary, but she did love the memorial her mother had designed. It was tucked away in the back of the cemetary surrounded by thick bushes, which bloomed beautiful purple flowers in the spring, and a tall cement wall. Inside the memorial was an elegant black marble angel, that stood about ten feet high. A black marble sitting bench was placed in the center. Marcus Verona would have appreciated what his beloved wife had done for him.

Shayna sat down on the Marble bench, and put her hands in her lap.

"Hi dad," she said, and began twiddling her thumbs. "You're not coming back for me, are you?" her eyes went to her hands, which were resting in her lap, "I'm scared, and the time is coming soon, I need you here." she closed her eyes and envisioned Cain. "I met someone," she said. "His name is Cain, and he's like you," she paused, "I guess. He said he would help me through this, I trust him. Also he..." Shayna was interrupted by a noise behind her, and quickly turned around. She was sitting on the bench with her back to the entrance of the memorial. As she turned, she saw tanned skin, and sandy brown hair. Derrick. The way he stood, looking at her gave her the creeps. He stared at her like she was a piece of meat. He always had, even when he was with Melina, but she had ignored it then.

Shayna stood up, and started walking toward the opening of the memorial to leave. She realized suddenly by the way he was standing, that he was intentionally blocking the entrance. She hastily looked around for another exit. The only way out was over the wall. She was trapped.

"Hi Derrick," she said, as she approached him.

"Where are you going Shayna?" he asked. "Don't leave."

"I have to go home," she said. She stood face to face with him, and was pretty sure he wasn't going to let her pass.

"I don't think you need to go anywhere," he said, and took a strand of her hair between his thumb and forefinger, and twisted it, like she did when nervous. His words were slurred, and he reeked of alcohol. My

God! She thought He's drunk! She shivered in disgust, she didn't want his dirty hands touching her at all.

"Come on Derrick, I have to go."

She tried to push past him. He grabbed her arm, and pulled her back.

"You're not going anywhere," he said.

She knew she was in trouble. She opened her mouth to scream, but Derrick's dirty, motor oil stained hand covered it. He enjoyed working on cars in his free time, which always left his hands soiled in oil.. He held her close to him, with her back against his chest.

"I always liked you better," he whispered into her ear.

He pushed her further into the memorials enclosure, where they were invisible behind the cement wall. Tears ran down Shayna's face uncontrollably. She couldn't believe what was happening.

When she felt the burning deep inside of her chest, she didn't know what to think. It was a sensation that she had never felt before. She could feel it building, almost boiling inside of her. Derrick turned her around so that she was facing him,and pushed her up against the angel statue. The angel's knee was digging into Shayna's back and was quite painful, with the weight of Derrick's body pushing on her. He put his hand on the back of her neck and leaned toward her with his mouth open.

Shayna knew she was going to explode. Something was happening inside of her. She didn't know what, but she wasn't scared, and she knew Derrick should be. He's going to die. She closed her eyes. She *was* going to explode. The deafening shriek that came next, reminded Shayna of a bird. Her eyes shot open, just as the massive hawk's razor sharp talons gripped the back of Derricks jacket, and ripped him away from her.

Throwing him across the memorial. The marble bench stopped his flight, and his body hit the ground hard, with a thud.

Shayna could see blood on his forehead and she became dizzy. She fell into, what was left of the snow, on her knees. Derrick laid unconscious a few feet away from her, and the hawk was long gone. She put her face in her hands and cried, rocking herself back and forth.

When she heard footsteps coming from behind her she didn't look up. She was too embarassed, she just cried. She felt strong hands on her upper arms.

"Shayna?" a soft musical voice said, "Are you okay?"

She cried harder. It was Cain. She was so grateful he was there. He turned her toward him, and she melted into his arms, burying her face in his chest, sobbing even harder.

"Let's get you out of here," he said, helping her to her feet, while still holding her close to him. He didn't ask what happened, he already knew.

"H…h…How did," she tried to choke back her sobs, "How did you know I was here?' she was finally able to get out.

"Aunt Mill sent me a message to come," he said walking her through the cemetary, "She said you were in danger, and to hurry."

Shayna didn't ask how Aunt Mill knew, everything was becoming so crazy to Shayna. She used her jacket sleeve to wipe the tears from her face. She didn't want to let go of Cain, but she needed to use her hands to try to staighten herself up before anyone else saw her.

"Are you okay?" he asked again.

She took a deep breath and exhaled slowly, "I will be." She looked up to the sky, "Thanks to some crazy hawk."

Cain looked at her quizically, "A hawk?" he said.
Shayna realized she was shaking, "Yes," she
answered.

"Hmmm…." Cain said and looked forward, and kept
walking.

They got to his car, and he opened the passenger
door for her, and helped her sit down.

"Stay here, I'll be right back."

Before Shayna could protest, Cain shut the door, and
headed back into the cemetary. He returned to the
BMW about five minutes later, but it felt like hours to
Shayna. She had halfway pulled herself together while
he was gone, and was anxious to get away from the
cemetary.

They pulled away from the curb, and she looked
back at the cemetary vowing to herself to never go
back. Her father's body wasn't there, so really, she had
no reason to return. Cain reached across the car and put
his hand on Shayna's knee.

"Is he dead?" she asked him.

"No. Unfortunately he will be fine," Cain looked at
Shayna and said, "Do you want him to be?"

"No. Yes. I mean, of course not." She wasn't sure
what outcome she wanted for Derrick. She knew she
didn't want to have to face him again, "What if he does
that to someone else? Or worse, already has?" she
asked Cain.

"He hasn't," he answered, matter of fact. "He was
drunk, and his attraction to you was too strong. He
couldn't control himself." He turned his head in
Shayna's direction, "He won't be drinking anymore
though."

"How do you know?" Shayna asked him, curious of
the answer.

"I impelled his mind. When he wakes up, he's going to think he wandered into the cemetary alone, and he won't even remember that you were here, or that he followed you."

"What about his injuries from being thrown by the hawk?" Shayna asked.What a mess. She thought.

"He'll probably just think that he got injured falling or something." Cain looked at Shayna concerned, "Are you *sure* you're okay?" he asked.

"Yes, I promise." She did not lie to him. She had been scared, but the fear had passed, and by the time Cain showed up, she was more afraid for Derrick. "Did you want to kill him?" she asked quietly.

Cain thought silently before answering, "I wanted to wipe him off the face of the earth. Drain him dry of every ounce of blood in his body. But I won't be responsible for killing a kid that just needs some good help," he said, and took his eyes away from the road to look at Shayna again. "I will kill him, if I ever catch him thinking unpure thoughts about you again. I knew I should have watched him better."

"What do you mean?" Shayna asked.

"A couple days ago at school, I passed him in the hallway, and he was thinking about you," Cain paused, he didn't want to finish, "He was thinking about you, undressed."

Shayna's stomach knotted up, she was going to be sick, "Pull over!" she cried, and Cain did.

"We can only stay for a little while," Cain said, and opened the door to the old farm house he lived in with Aunt Mill. They stepped into the foyer, "But, then I will need to get you home." He needed to feed, and didn't want Shayna there while he did. He knew it was ridiculous to be embarassed, but he couldn't help to not be. "Can I get you anything? A drink or something?" he asked her.

"Yeah," she said, and smiled, "Make it stiff."

It took Cain a second to realize she was only joking. He smiled at her humor, and excused himself.

"I'll be right back. You can have a seat, if, you'd like," he told her, and walked into what she guessed, was the kitchen.

Shayna didn't want to sit. She looked around the foyer, and the living room. There were a lot of pictures of Aunt Mill and what was probably her family, a large family, full of mostly women, but none of Cain. Of course not, Shayna thought. The inside of the farm house was decorated beautifully. Everything seemed so old, but very well kept. There was an old grandfathers clock in a corner of the living room by the fireplace, which Shayna thought was at least a hundred years old. In the opposite corner there stood a globe of the world that looked as though it could be from as early as the fifteenth century. If they even knew the earth was round then. She thought, and laughed to herself. Everything was so fascinating. A collection Shayna thought must have taken years to acquire.

Cain returned with a glass of sweet tea for Shayna. Aunt Mill was from the south and always had some around.

"How's Sid?" Shayna asked, after taking a long drink.

"I think I need to just keep him in the barn for a while. So he stays put," he answered, "Although, he'll probably figure out a way out of his stall too."

"Can we go see him?" she asked.

She had never met another horse quite like Obsidion. She never realized a horse could have so much personality, and Obsidion was full of it. She was axious to see him.

Cain stood up from the chair he was seated in, "Of course," he said.

He reached for Shayna's hand, to help her up from the couch. She smiled at him freely when their eyes locked, and he brushed a strand of stray hair away from her face, tucked it behind her ear and asked one last time, "Are you sure you're okay?"

"Thanks to you, and the hawk, I'll be fine," she answered.

"But, I didn't do anything," he pointed out.

"But you were going to," she told him, as they made their way to the front door. "And, if you hadn't shown up, I would probably still be sitting on the ground, in the cemetary, a total mess," she paused and thought back, "What was he going to do to me?" she asked Cain.

"You know what he was going to do," Cain said. He felt he should give her a little bit of a warning to what could happen to her, "And, for you, it would probably be the worst pain imaginable."

"Why?" Shayna was curious. She knew she would probably be told things that she wouldn't want to hear, but she needed to know also.

"Because of who you are, Shayna Verona." He hated having to be the one to have to tell her such things. Her father should have done this. He thought.

When Cain had come to Interlochen, his agenda had not included tutoring, and falling in love with her. It had been the exact opposite. But here they were walking hand in hand, toward his barn, and he knew he would probably tell her almost anything she wanted to know. Almost.

"You don't seem to understand. You're not just any Halfling Princess." He said Halfling Princess while putting two fingers up on each hand, to make quotation marks. "Your father was a very special kind of vampire. No one created him, he just was. Maybe he was born that way, maybe it was a natural transformation," Cain said, and shrugged his shoulders, "Who knows."

They walked through the tall double doors of the barn, and Shayna could hear a loud banging, and knew it was Obsidion kicking his stall. She smiled, and let Cain continue, as they headed down the corridor to the stalls.

"Your blood is so unbelievably strong and pure because of your father. I don't think I've ever heard of another princess like you. That's why I don't really know how your change will go," he said, and looked at the ground, embarrassed, by what he was about to say to her, "But I do know that if you lose your virginity before your change, not only will it hurt horribly, but your blood will be tainted."

Shayna thought about what he was saying. How does he know so much about me? She wondered. But she didn't care. In a way, she was glad that she didn't have to keep her secrets from him.

"Tainted?" she whispered to no one.

Obsidion pressed his muzzle to the bars, when they walked up, and Shayna rubbed his soft, velvety nose.

"Hey Sid," she said and gave his nose a kiss between his big nostrils. "You ready for tomorrow? I am"

She looked at Cain briefly, and then returned her attention to the horse. She had more questions for Cain, but had decided to wait until their ride the next day, when there was less stress. She had taken in enough for one day. Cain watched Shayna and Obsidion in pure admiration of how two creatures could be so perfectly beautiful together. He didn't care what anyone, or any*thing,* had to say about it. They were *both* his.

Before he could stop himself, he grabbed Shayna by the wrist with one hand. With the other, he placed it on the back of her neck and pulled her to him, and pressed his lips to hers. Hard, passionately.

Once again Shayna's knees went weak. Cain held her up, and kissed her harder. Shayna's body trembled with goosebumps. To say she had butterflies in her stomach, would be putting it mildly. His lips were cold, and he tasted like sweet fruit to her. She returned his kiss eagerly. Something was happening because of this kiss. She knew, when Cain found a bale of hay and sat them both down, that it was happening to him too. He held her tighter, and kissed her harder. Niether one could pull away from each other, even if they had wanted to. Eventually they seemed to be fused together. Shayna had never kissed anyone before this. Besides Noah, and that was, well that was Noah. But she knew, a kiss didn't feel like this. Cain ran his hand through her hair at the back of her neck, and slowly began to pull away. Gently he traced Shayna's lips with his tongue.

Shayna, out of breath, was barely able to get out, "What was that?" She felt paralyzed in his arms, but didn't want to move anyway, she was where she belonged.

Cain gazed deeply into her eyes, and held her even tighter, just barely squeezing her too hard.

"I don't know, my Princess, I have never felt anything like that before."

"Was that supposed to happen?" she asked, putting her hand on his chest. She was a little worried, but nonetheless, wanting to kiss him again.

"Whether it was supposed to happen or not, it did. I just hope there are no unforeseen consequences, to whatever that was," Cain said. He too was a little worried, but tried not to show it. He thought the kiss was truly phenominal.

"That's what I worry about, unforeseen consequences," Shayna told him, "But," she said lying her head on his shoulder, "That was amazing."

Cain's throat burned. Her kiss had tasted so wonderful, he was losing it. He could still taste her.

"I have to get you home," he said suddenly.

Shayna noticed the same look in his eyes, that she saw the day at school, when she ran into him coming out of the bathroom.

"Is everything alright?" she asked. She felt so perfect in his arms, she didn't want to leave.

Suddenly, Cain got up, and stood Shayna on her feet too.

"It will be. I just have to get you out of here." He took her hand, and began to lead her out of the barn.

She didn't try to stop him. It was his place, and he was one hundred times stronger than her. But she was confused.

"Cain, did I do something wrong?" she asked, taken aback, "I don't understand."

He stopped and turned, facing her. Rings of red encircled his emerald green eyes. Shayna's lips parted a little, in perplexity.

"What don't you understand Shayna?" He was angry, but not with her. "I am a vampire, that craves blood, and you are still human. A human with the most amazing blood, any vampire has ever caught scent of." He paused, he didn't want her to think he was angry with her, "Every second I am with you, is a constant battle to control my instincts." His immortal eyes pleaded with her, "So, please Shayna."

She didn't say a word. She continued forward, and Cain took the lead, all but running out of the barn. Seeing his extended canines, behind his beautiful mouth, had excited Shayna. She knew she was in danger.

They reached Cain's car and he opened the driver door, and gestured for Shayna to get in, placing his keys in her hand.

"What?" She couldn't believe it, "No!"

"Just be back in the morning for our ride. Everything will be fine," he said with solace. He took her hand knowing he was putting her at further risk, by keeping her close. "I'll see you in the morning Princess. Goodnight."

He kissed her forehead softly. His lips tingled when they made contact with her skin. He helped her into the car, and closed the door, waving her to go.

Shayna fumbled with the keys, trying to find an ignition key. She found one and gave it a try. The BMW purred to life. She looked up, Cain was gone. She took a deep breath and put the car into gear. She asked herself how she was going to explain this to Sarah. To Melina. To anyone. She pulled onto the highway and away from the farm house. She didn't want to bring his car home, but she hadn't been given a choice. What was she thinking?

Chapter 6

Shayna sat on the porch swing at her house for twenty minutes, soaking up the day, and thinking about everything that was happening. There was so much to absorb and process. Cain was her angel, or better yet, her Prince. He was the best thing that had entered her life, since her father's "death" and she knew, that with Cain by her side, she could conquer anything.

She finally decided to go inside, and she opened the front door to a house, that was slowly darkening.

"Who's snazzy car?" She heard her mother ask. Shayna wasn't quite sure where she was, in their large Victorian house.

"A friends," she answered. She listened for a reply, to decipher where her mother was. The only light on in the house was a small table lamp in the living room.

"Mmm Hmm," she heard.

Top of the stairs, Shayna realized. She looked up, her mothers silhouette stood at the top of the stairs.

"Is it the new boy?" Sarah asked.

"He's not just a boy," Shayna didn't know what else to say. She knew her mother wasn't ignorant. Sarah knew her daughter well.

Sarah came down the stairs, and stood with her daughter. She tucked Shayna's hair behind her ear.

"That's what worries me. I don't want you to throw away everything that you've worked so hard for, because of a boy or anyone." Sarah told her daughter.

"Mom, it's not like that," Shayna said. They walked to the living room, and sat down on the couch together, "He would never let me neglect my responsibilities."

"I guess I'm worried, also because I have never seen you fall for anyone like this. It's not like you. But," Sarah sighed, "I know that you can't help how your heart feels, love is a powerful emotion."

"Mom!" Shayna blurted, "Who said anything about love? I just met him on Monday."

"Shayna, I see it all over your face." Sarah smiled, and squeezed Shayna's hand, "You can deny it if you want, but I haven't seen this kind of happiness in your eyes, since you were a little girl."

Sarah knew that she would have to let go of her daughters one day, but she had always hoped she would be able to hold on to Shayna a little longer, than it was looking like she was going to. She knew that when Shayna left, that she would possibly never come back.

"I just want to make sure you know what you are doing, Shay. *You* have too much to lose."

"Mom, I promise. I know what I am doing, and I promise that I won't lose sight of my life's goals.

Sarah smiled, "I know, I'm sorry, I worry too much. You are a smart girl. I know you know what you are doing," she said. Sarah trusted Shayna's judgement more than Melina's most of the time. "So, tell me about this boy," she said changing the subject, "When do I get to meet him?"

"His name is Cain," Shayna began, not realizing the grin that had spread across her face, "He lives at the one huge farmhouse with the big white barn, and like ten different horse pastures. Near Karlin. You know where

I'm talking about right?" she asked. Sarah nodded her head, and Shayna continued, "He lives there with his aunt. They moved here from California, and they opened up a little bookstore near Interlochen Corner's." Shayna beamed at her mother, "Anything else?"

"When do I get to meet him?" she said with an inflexible look.

"Seriously?" Shayna asked. "I'm still getting to know him myself, but soon. Okay?"

"Promise?" Sarah said.

"Yes," Shayna promised, "I'm going on a ride with him tomorrow."

Sarah interrupted Shayna before she could go any further, "What happened to, Mom, can I go on a ride with him?" she asked caustically, "And what kind of ride is he taking you on?"

Shayna smirked at her mother, and cocked her head to the side, "Mom. Can I go horseback riding with Cain tomorrow?"

"Thank you Shayna. Yes you can go," Sarah responded, "Of course you can go. But I want to meet him when you come home."

"Yes Ma'am," Shayna said, and kissed her Sarah's cheek, "Thank you mom, for understanding."

"That's what I'm here for Shay," Sarah hugged Shayna, and inhaled her scent. She thought to herself that Shayna always smelled good, "Now go get your phone, it's been ringing all day. You're supposed to keep it with you," she said, "Isn't that the point of having it?" she was trying to be the parent again.

"Okay, okay," Shayna got up and headed toward the stairs, "Mom?" Shayna stopped and turned around. Maybe I should tell her. She thought, "Nevermind," she said and bounded up the stairs, leaving Sarah alone on the couch.

Shayna went into her room and grabbed her phone off the dresser, where she had left it that morning. She already knew it was Noah who had been calling, but when she looked at her phone to her surprise, most of the calls had been from a blocked number.

There was a knock on the door, and Sarah poked her head in, "By the way," she said, "Why are you so dirty?"

Shayna looked down at herself. Her jeans were covered in mud. She knew the mud was from the cemetary, but she could never tell Sarah what happened. She tried to come up with something quickly.

"I was helping Cain with his horses. The melting snow made a pretty muddy mess out of the pastures." She hated lying, especially to her mother, but this time she felt it was for the best. She wanted to just forget the whole thing.

"Well get cleaned up, and I'll make dinner," Sarah told her.

Sarah closed the door, and Shayna took a pair of baby blue flannel pajama pants, and a white T-shirt, out of her dresser, and went to the bathroom to take a shower. She took off her shirt in the bathroom, and she gasped in shock. Her bloodstone was gone. She hoped and prayed it was at Cain's house, or in his car, but her instinct told her it was in the cemetery.

"I don't want to go back there," she said to the reflection in the mirror. She stared at the face looking back at her. I am a vampire. She thought. I shouldn't be afraid or intimidated by some creep. "I am a vampire" she whispered, shaking her head.

She decided to wait until Sunday to go back and find it. If that was truly where it was. She was over the fear of it all, but was definitely not ready to go back just yet.

She turned on the shower, and finished undressing. She adjusted the water temperature, and she stepped in. The hot water felt good on her bare skin. She closed her eyes, and let the water flow all over her body.

After a dinner of bloody steak, potatoes, and salad, Shayna went upstairs to call Noah. He didn't answer, and she didn't blame him. She *had* been ignoring him, when she could have at least called and told him what was going on with Cain. She wasn't trying to *not* tell and she wasn't embarassed. She just wanted to be able to process things a little more, without his influence or anyone else's for that matter.

She turned off her bedside lamp, and lie back on the bed. She closed her eyes. She was anticipating the day to come. She lay in the dark room for about a half an hour before her mind went blank, and the dream took over.

Shayna took in a deep breath, and entered her father's memorial. She wanted to find her necklace, and leave immediately. When she saw the figure on the marble sitting bench, she stopped.

"Don't be scared," a very familiar voice said, "It's me."

The figure looked up at her, and Shayna gasped.

"Daddy!" she ran to her father, and all but knocked him off of the sitting bench with her embrace.

"Take it easy Shay," he said to her.

"I missed you so much," she cried, tears uncontrollably flowing down her face.

"Shayna." He put his hands on her shoulders, and sat her down on the bench, "You need to listen. This is a dream, but I am really here. I'm coming to you the only way that I know how." Shayna gave her father an understanding nod, and he continued. "I know you know what you are now. I can tell by the way you carry, and present yourself," he said. She nodded again, "I have sent someone to help you. To guide you, and protect you during this transition. You can trust him, I knew him for many years."

Shayna smiled at the thought of this, "*You* sent him?"

"He's already here?" Her father's eyes narrowed, "I didn't know. How long has he been here?" he asked.

"Are you coming back?" she asked softly, ignoring his question, but not really wanting the answer to hers.

Marcus Verona put a soft, cold hand on his daughters cheek.

"No," he answered, "I'm not."

A single tear fell from Shayna's cheek, "I didn't think so," she muttered.

Her father stood up and looked around, "This memorial is beautiful," he said. "Sarah did an astonishing job." He walked up to the angel statue, running his fingers down her wings, "It is a shame my body isn't here."

"Where is it?" Shayna asked, "What happened?"

"Gone," he replied, "Burnt to ash."

"What? How?"

"Someone who held a grudge," he answered. More tears came, he grabbed her shoulders again, and looked her in the eyes, "Shayna, you need to be strong. You are, and will be, a very special being," he said, "I know you are going to make me proud to have been your father."

"I just miss you so much," she sniffled, "When I found that letter, it gave me hope that you would be back for me."

"I will try to visit you this way, as often as I can make it possible. But, in the meantime, know that you will be taken care of," he said this, and his image started to become hazy, and began fading away.

"No, Daddy, don't go," Shayna cried, tears pouring down her face, "Don't go."

Chapter 7

Shayna did not want any interrogations from Melina, and was thankful that she had stayed the night at Delany's house. She had asked Sarah not to say anything to Melina about the car, and Sarah had promised that she wouldn't. As long as Shayna took her cell phone with her. She left the house to go to Cain's, with the phone, but she powered it off as soon as she was in the car. She didn't want the day to be interrupted by a ringing phone.

She pulled into Cain's driveway and smiled when she saw him in the property's outdoor arena, lunging Obsidion. Cain looked up and saw her, and began to slow Obsidion to a walk, pulling the magnificent horse closer to him, as he did. Shayna got out of the car and walked to the arena, and Cain led Obsidion out toward her.

"Good morning," she said to him as they approached each other.

"Morning," Cain returned the greeting, "I wasn't sure you would come back after last night, but I am glad you did," he said.

"Well I had to return your car," she joked.

He smiled at her. He couldn't get over how beautiful she was.

"Are you okay?" he asked.

"I am." She was finally able to not think about the previous days events, so much.

Cain smiled and nodded at her. Knowing how strong, and fearless she seemed to be.

He handed Shayna Obsidions reins, and said, "I'll go grab Glytter, the horse I'll be riding. She's tied up in the barn. I'll just be a moment."

"Okay," Shayna said. She stroked Obsidion's muzzle as Cain walked to the barn. "Are you as anxious as I am?" she asked the horse, "Now let's see if I can get on you, without his help,"

Shayna stepped back and looked at the large horse. He was all decked out in black leather tack, that was trimmed with silver. He looked even bigger than she remembered, with the small English saddle he bore on his back. Just when Shayna thought there was no way she would be able to climb up on him alone, without delay, Obsidion stretched out one of his front legs and bent the other, so that he was kneeling down.

Shayna stared at the horse in disbelief, "Did you just read my mind?" she asked him in amazement.

Obsidion huffed and threw his head up. Shayna didn't hesitate, she immediately climbed on his back and Obsidion righted himself as Cain appeared, leading a beautiful bay mare that was nearly as big as Obsidion. She had decided not to tell Cain about what Sid had done. It would be their secret, and she hoped she wasn't just imagining it. This horse is amazing. She thought.

"I thought you couldn't get a saddle on him?" she asked Cain, when he approached with his horse.

"You know," he started, "It was so weird. When I came to get him, he never fought me. He did everything willingly, like he knew it was for you." He gathered his horses reins and pulled himself up into her saddle, "It looks like he is, as crazy about you, as I am!" With that

Cain yelled out, and gave the mare a kick in her side, and she took off towards the trees.

Shayna gathered Sid's reins, squeezed his sides and told him, with her mind, to run and to run fast. The horse didn't hesitate. As soon as Shayna had projected her thoughts to him, he was off in the direction of the trees. Within seconds they were running next to Cain and Glytter.

"He is a beautiful animal," Cain said to her, "But he belongs to you." He slowed his horse to a walk, and Obsidion slowed too, at Shayna's silent command. "I don't know at all, what he or you are thinking, but I can definitely sense that there is a connection between the two of you."

The horses walked side by side, on a trail, that was surrounded by pine trees.

"You didn't happen to find my fathers necklace anywhere, did you?" she asked him, hoping the answer would be yes.

"No," he said, "I'm sorry, I didn't."

"I think I have an idea of where I lost it," she told him, and sighed quietly, "I'll have to go there and look tomorrow." She knew he would know where she thought it was. She didn't have to tell him.

Cain did know, "Do you want me to go with you?" he asked, thinking she wouldn't want to go alone.

She looked at him, smiling at the gesture, "I think I need to go back alone. I didn't want to *ever* go back, and now that I know I have to I feel like I should do it alone. I think I'll be okay," she said, believing herself.

Cain understood how she felt, "Very well," he simply said.

Shayna told Obsidion to trot ahead in her special way, and he immediately obeyed. She wasn't sure of the trail they were on, but she trusted Obsidion not to lead her into danger. She wanted to forget about what had happened in the cemetary, but it seemed to be impossible.

"Shayna," Cain called ahead to her, "I want you to know something."

He wanted her to know exactly *why*, he was such a danger to her. He needed her to understand. But when Obsidion turned back toward him and looked at him like Cain was talking to *him* and he saw Shayna's beautiful face, eyes focused on him and full of happiness, he couldn't do it. He couldn't ruin the moment she was in. He would save it for another day. His mind raced for something to say to her instead, he finally said the only thing he could come up with.

"Shayna," he began, "I want you to know that he is yours," Cain pointed at Obsidion. "He belongs to you now. I believe he was meant for you."

The look in Shayna's eyes was all that Cain needed as a 'thank you'.

"What?" she asked, dismayed, "Are you kidding me?"

"Well, I can't do anything with him," he said, catching up to Shayna and Sid again, "He hates me."

"That's not true. He seemed just fine with you earlier," she told him. She didn't want to take his horse from him.

"Only because somehow, this damn horse knew you were coming." He was frustrated thinking about it, "I don't how, but he knew."

"I agree, there is something between us for sure," she told him, "But, are you sure?"

Cain nodded his head, "Yes," he said.

"Wow. Okay. I guess I can't really argue," she said. The horses were close enough for them to touch and Shayna reached out and took Cain's hand.

"Thank you," she told him. "You don't know how much this means to me."

"Trust me. I might not know what's on your mind or that horses." His ice cold hand squeezed hers gently, "But I can *see* how much it means to you."

"The only problem is, that I don't have a place to keep him," she said this, knowing the response she would receive, and smiled at him.

"Well," he said, and smiled back at her, "I have to get you out to my place somehow. Don't I?"

"That's right," she said, with a laugh. "So, where are you taking me?" she asked him. She had begun to become more curious. She didn't think there were very many places he could take her, that she hadn't already been to in this area.

"I told you, you'll see," he said, with a mischievious smile.

His dark hair was falling around his face and his eyes caught every bit of light, and reflected it back out like a gemstone. God, he's gorgeous! She thought. She didn't care where he was taking her, she would go anywhere with him.

"Fine," she said, "Can I ask you some questions then?"

"You can ask me anything Shayna, and I will try to answer the best that I can," he told her. Although he was a little nervous. He knew she was very inquisitive as to who she was, and he knew, he was walking a fine line.

"Okay," she began. The horses led the way, they seemed to be on a game path, and the horses were following it on their own. "I don't know where to start. I have so much to ask, but I don't know what to ask first," she sighed in frustration. The sun began to peek through the trees at them, and she took it as a cue, "The sun," she said, "What does it do to us?"

"Didn't you read the book you bought?" he asked with a smirk.

"How did you know I bought that book?" she asked. She hadn't thought that Aunt Mill would tell him, and she still believed she hadn't. He couldn't enter her mind. So how? She didn't have anything to hide anymore, but she was curious how he knew.

"I do the inventory," Cain said, "I assisted the only other two customers in that day, and they didn't buy it. So, I knew it was you."

"Oh," she said, blushing a little. "Well, to tell the truth. I just skimmed through it. Mainly to find out, if I had to spend my days in the dark," she laughed quietly, "You know what I mean?"

"Do I!" He nodded his head. He had spent the first seven months of his immortal existance hiding from the sun, until he found out about bloodstones. "Well, the sun does do *something* to us…" Before he could finish, Shayna interrupted him.

"It doesn't make our skin sparkle does it?" she asked laughing.

"Sorry. No," he laughed himself a little, at her joke, "But it does burn us." He saw Shayna's eyes widen, and thought twice about continuing. He didn't want to frighten her, but he knew she needed to know. He wished, he would of had someone to teach him about the life he lived, "You won't turn to ash and die immediately, unless you're stupid enough to stand in it for an excessive amount of time," he said, and waited for her to ease up and relax a little before he went on, "It *will* burn your skin though, it reddens and blisters pretty bad."

"Like a sunburn?" Shayna asked.

"Yes," he answered, "But a really bad instant sun burn, that is noticeable within minutes."

"And my bloodstone will protect me?"

"Yes, if you find it." He would give her one of his if she was unable to find it, but he sensed that she would.

"Okay next question," she said, moving away from the subject of the cemetary again, "How did you become a vampire?"

Cain tried to think of a way to tell her without lying to her, and without telling her his secret to early.

After a few silent moments he said, "Someone tried to kill me, and a vampire changed me right before I actually died."

The horses started up a hill, leaving the path behind them. "I can't imagine anyone wanting to kill *you*," Shayna said to him.

Cain closed his eyes, briefly, thinking back to that night.

"It was a stranger," he said, "I was attacked from behind one night, while returning home from attending errands for my father," Shayna could see the pain in his eyes as he spoke. "I loved my family, I was of noble blood, and it was a big ordeal when I disappeared. I refused to go home to them. I was different, and they would have known it."

"So you never saw your family again?" she asked, sad for him.

"No," he said softly, but not truthfully.

There was one family member that he continued to see after his mortal death, but Cain wanted to keep this person a secret from Shayna as long as he could. He knew and feared, that it was only a matter of time before she found out.

"Will it be that way with me?" Shayna asked him. It made her sad to think of not seeing her family. She had thought about it a lot, since she found out she would be a vampire.

"It doesn't *have* to be," he said, "But, they would know you were different, and you would constantly have to battle your instincts not to kill them," he looked at her knowing this was all very hard for her, "It's best that you at least leave here, until you know how to control yourself."

"Will you go with me?" she asked him.

He looked into her eyes and said, "Nothing would make me happier Princess," he knew how hard things would be for her, and he wanted to be there for her to make everything as easy as possible for her, "You know Shayna, I didn't ask for this life, and if I had been given a choice that night, I would have chose to die." Cain became quiet, he was lost in thought, thinking about the past, and thinking about the night he changed. Finally he said, "Shayna up until I saw you for the very first time. I had always wished that I *had* died that night. But now, I believe you were my reason for carrying on. No one has ever made me feel, the way that I feel when I am with you," Cain couldn't believe that he was revealing his soul to her. He couldn't help it. He knew he could tell her this, and definitely not ruin her day.

They had come down another hill, and Shayna had decided she was officially lost. She had lost track of what direction they were heading in, after the horses had crossed the highway. She knew then, that they were heading east, but she stopped paying attention after that.

"Why did you want to die?" she asked, as they followed a creek into a gully. She didn't understand. She would be lying to herself if she said the thought of living forever, didn't excite her a little.

"I never wanted this Shayna," he said. She saw him wince as if in pain, "Up until this moment, I believed that this was not my true fate, and that I should have died that night." He drew in a deep breath, although breathing was unnecessary for him. He was breathing her in. "But seeing you sitting on that horse right now, I know that *you* are my fate."

The horses had been making their way up a hill, and before Shayna could respond to Cain, they reached the top, and came out onto a bluff that looked out over, what Shayna knew, was the Manistee River.

"Isn't it beautiful?" Cain asked her.

Shayna knew of this place well, she had heard about it all her life, but had never came in person until he had brought her.

"It's called the High Rollaway," she said, staring down at the river, which looked like a horse shoe, from the top of the bluff. It rolled in, around a bend and rolled back out, disappearing from veiw, "I hear it's absolutely beautiful in the fall."

Noah pulled up to Shayna's house around noon, and parked his purple El Camino at the curb. She better be here! He thought, while waliking up to the door. The Prelude was parked in the driveway, but that never meant Shayna was home, Melina always had it. Shayna preferred to walk whenever she could.

After two knocks, Melina answered the door.

"What's up Noah?" she asked him, and leaned against the door frame, fidgiting with her straight blonde hair.

"Hey kiddo," he said, and winked at her. "Where's Shayna?"

"Seriously?" Melina said, "You don't know?"

"No," Noah said, shaking his head in confusion.

"She's with Cain."

"What?!" Noah was flabergasted. He knew Shayna liked this *new kid*, but he couldn't believe that she was already out with him. "Already?" he asked. "I thought she would at least take her time."

"Yeah right!" Melina laughed, "Are you kidding? They've been inseparable since Wednesday, or at least it seems that way," she told him, "It's kinda weird."

"No wonder," Noah said under his breath.

"What?"

"She hasn't answered my calls, or called me back, or anything," Noah said, and sat down on the porch swing the twin's father had put up, the year he "died". "I thought she was upset with me, but now I see she has traded me in for a better model," Noah said, with a pout.

Noah valued his friendship with Shayna dearly. He thought of her as a sister. He thought she was attractive, very attractive. But he knew he wasn't the one she needed, and he accepted that, and settled for being her best friend.

"Nah," Melina said and, came outside to sit next to him on the swing, "You're a classic, she would never trade you in," she smiled at him, he was always upbeat, and funny, and cared about his friendship with her sister. Melina could see why Shayna would rather be around Noah, over anyone else…until she had met Cain, "So what brings you by?" Melina asked Noah.

Noah leaned back against the red pinstriped swing cushion, feeling a little frustrated, "Well, Shayna was supposed to go to Traverse City with me today," he said, "To help me pick out a tux for the Winter Formal." Noah looked at Melina with an idea, he was going to Traverse City regardless, but he wanted a females opinion, "Do you want to go?" he asked Melina, with raised eyebrows.

"To help you pick out a tux?"

Noah nodded his head and smiled.

Melina wasn't sure what to say, normally she didn't hang out with Noah, or anyone else besides her "Girls", but she thought it might be fun, and said "Sure let's go."

"Cool," Noah said. He was a little surprised, but glad nonetheless.

"Let me grab my bag, and put on my shoes," Melina stood up.

"I'll be in my car/" Noah also stood up, and headed toward his El Camino.

When Melina climbed into the El Camino after getting her things, she immediately filled the small cab of the car with the aroma of what could only be Calvin Klein.

"So I have to tell you something Noah," she said closing the door, "I love your car." This was something that Melina would never admit to anyone again. If Noah told anyone, she would say he was lying.

The purple car had black, gold trimmed, lightening bolts on the sides, and the inside was all black leather, with a fuzzy black dash, and two Purple dice hanging from the rearview mirror.

"Why, thank you Melina," Noah said, and pulled away from the curb, "I like it too," he reached up, and stroked the dash, petting it.

Melina laughed at this, but thought of Shayna, "Noah," she said, changing the subject, "I am a little worried about Shay."

"Wait what?" He was fumbling through radio stations, and she had caught him off guard. He had never heard the words *Shayna* and *worried* in the same sentence before. "Why?" he asked.

"What do you mean, why?" Melina had never really paid much attention to what Shayna was doing until now, and she thought Shayna was definitely stepping out of her normal comfort zone when it came to this boy Cain. Melina didn't understand what was so special about him to Shayna, besides his good looks and obvious money, which Melina knew wouldn't attract Shayna. "Has she ever stood you up before?" she asked Noah.

Noah looked at Melina sitting on the other side of the car, he knew she had a point.

"No," he answered.

"She hasn't even known him a week," Melina said, "And she leaves for a walk, and he brings her home. This morning when I got home, the neighbor asked me if we were getting a new car. When I said no, he said he didn't think us girls would be getting a brand new Beemer anyway. He said it was at our house all night."

"Wait what?!" Noah couldn't believe what he was hearing, "He stayed the night with her? Where was your mom?"

"Mom said Shayna drove his car home," Melina told him.

Noah scratched his head. This *was* odd behavior for Shayna, he thought. Do you think he has her brainwashed or something?" he asked, turning on to US 131.

"Is that even possible Noah?" she said looking at him with raised eyebrows, "Really?"

Shayna didn't want the day to end, but she knew eventually, they would have to make the long ride, back to Interlochen. Cain had not only brought her somewhere, she had never been to before, but while they walked around the area they had found a hotspring that Shayna was sure no one knew was there. If they did, they weren't telling.

She had learned so much about Cain. He had been born in a city in Tuscany, Italy. He told about it's beautiful cathedrals, and gardens. He told her about the places he had been to and, people he had met, like Queen Elizabeth, Abraham Lincoln, and Martin Luther King Jr. He told her about things he had seen in his many years. She learned a lot, but she got the feeling that he was holding back something. She felt though, that if he was holding back something, that he must have a good reason. She didn't want to push it, so she let it go.

They sat in the hot spring directly across from each other. Shayna couldn't believe that the place existed, and no one in the area knew about it. It was so beautiful. Cain had come prepared with towels, and something for Shayna to eat, and water to drink, in Glytter's saddle bag. He reached across the pool for Shayna's hand, when she took his, he pulled her to him through the water. They had taken off their clothes and were using their underwear as bathing suits. When Shayna was close enough to him, he wrapped his arms around her, and held her close to his body. Shayna couldn't help but notice, that even in the hot spring, his body was ice cold.

He looked deep into her eyes, so that she would see how serious he was, and said, "Shayna, I want to spend the rest of eternity with you. I want to live for you, or at least exist, for you. I am a very determined soul, and I won't be happy, unless you are happy." He gently held her face in his hands, and cautiously placed his lips to hers, preparing for what would come.

The instant their lips touched the electrical sensation infused them together. Cain pressed his lips harder to hers. The pool began to bubble more rapidly around them, and the birds that were in the trees, flew off in a frenzied flock. The only thing either of them could do, was hold each other tighter, kiss each other harder, and ride out the euphora of their kiss. When the bubbles in the hot spring subsided, and returned to normal, they were finally able to break the spell that bound them together.

Again breathless, and gasping for air, Shayna asked, "Is that going to happen every time we kiss?"

"I hope so," Cain answered, still holding her. "That is the most amazing feeling I've had in three hundred years." He stroked her hair, and said softly, "I'm guessing that it's not a coincedence, and that there is something behind it."

They stayed in the hot spring, in each others arms. Talking, holding each other, and kissing for the rest of the afternoon. Each time they kissed the sensation grew stronger, and their feelings for each other more passionate. They packed up their horses and headed west in the direction of Interlochen, in a world of ecstacy and more in love with each other, than both thought was possible.

Chapter 8

Shayna walked through the cemetary gates, and anxiety swept through her. She began to tremble. When she had fallen asleep, she was lost in the most amazing day she had ever had, but when she awoke, she had a feeling and a sense of change, something new. Something big.

She walked past some headstones and she saw a vision of someone waiting for her. She couldn't see a face, only a dark figure. The closer she got to her father's memorial, the more she was sure there was someone waiting for her. She could feel it. A flood of emotions flowed through her body at once. Happiness, sadness, terror, and worry.

She took a deep breath and walked behind a large tomb, toward the memorial garden. Reaching the entrance, she closed her eyes, and said a quiet, short prayer. She opened her eyes, and stepped into the garden. Immediately her eyes focused on the figure leaning against the dark angel. Her father's bloodstone swinging back and forth from it's chain in his hand. Shayna gasped in wonderment. A new wave of emotions flooded her, and she did not know whether to run to him, or from him.

"Lose something?" he asked. His beautiful face forming a smile. "I thought you might be back for it."

"It's you," she was able to say, "How is it you?" Shayna thought she was dreaming. He was so perfect. Everything about him was the same as she remembered, even his voice. She was frozen. She wanted to run to him, but something in her mind kept her where she was. "How?"

"I told you," he said, taking a step toward her. Warily she took a step back. "I'm getting closer, and now I'm close enough, I'm here."

Shayna's mind was racing, a feeling she was beginning to get used to. Before even realizing she was thinking it, she said, "My father sent you, didn't he?"

A little surprised that she knew, he answered, "As a matter of fact he did. He thought I could be of assistance to you."

"You're a little late," she told him, daring to take a step further into the enclosure of the memorial. She laughed a little at what she was about to say, "I've met someone else."

"So it appears," he laughed a her joke. They stood face to face. "Your father sent me to protect you from creeps like him."

He placed the necklace in the palm of Shayna's hand, and closed his hand around hers.

"He's not a creep," she said defensivly, "He would never hurt me."

The mysteriuos boy let out a rumbling laugh, "Shayna, Shayna, Shayna," he said. "You are so naïve, you know nothing of Cain."

"How do you know his name?" she asked, "And what is yours?"

He touched her cheek lightly and whispered, "Shayna, I know more about him, than you ever will," he traced his fingers down her neck, and across her collarbone. "My, you truly are a lovely creature," he stood back examining her.

In the three years that Shayna had dreamed about this boy, and fallen in love with him, he had only spoken once, and now that he stood in front of her, she was both a little intimidated, and excited by how cocky he seemed to be. He circled around her, looking her up and down. She saw him lick his lips and she knew at that moment, that he too, was a vampire.

"Your name," she demanded again. She had many questions, but at that moment and for the last three years, she only wanted a name.

He took in a deep breath, and she knew that he was breathing in her scent. He looked down and when she saw his eyes again, there was a familiar red ring around his pupils.

"Aiden," he whispered to her, "Aiden Luca."

He took her hand again and kissed it gently with soft cold lips. He released her hand and began walking backwards, until he was about ten feet away from her.

"And I will show you why he is such a creep."

Before he had finished speaking, he leapt into the air, and with an explosion of feathers the hawk appeared and soared into the sky. Shayna watched him fly until he was out of sight. She plopped down on the marble bench, dumbfounded.

"Luca," she said quietly to herself, "Is he Cain's...brother?"

The first thing Shayna saw, when she walked through the front door was Melina sitting on the couch, with a large grin on her face. Shayna had managed to avoid her for most of the weekend, but knew she would have to face her eventually.

"Sup, Shay?" Melina asked.

"Sup, Mel?"

"Why don't you tell me *Miss Beemer*?" Melina teased.

Melina wanted as much information from Shayna as possible, but she knew that Shayna would tell her very little, if anything. She would accept anything she could get.

"Mom said she wouldn't tell!" Shayna accused.

Melina didn't want to *out* her mother for only verifying, what she already suspected.

"She didn't," Melina tried to smile convincingly at Shayna.

"Alright Mel," Shayna sighed, and plopped down in her favorite chair in the livingroom, across from Melina, "Let's get this over with. What do you want to know."

"Really?!" Melina beemed. She couldn't believe that Shayna was caving so easily. "Anything?"

"No," Shayna said, "Of course not *anything*."

"Hmm," Melina thought hard, "Okay. How did he get you so wrapped around his finger?" she asked.

"What?" Shayna knew having this conversation with Melina was a bad idea. "I am *not* wrapped around his finger," she defended herself.

"Oh, puhlease," Melina said, with a snickered. "For the last week you have spent every spare second with him. I know you Shayna, this isn't normal for you."

Shayna rolled her eyes.

"Oh by the way," Melina added, "I went with Noah to get his tuxedo yesterday."

Shayna jumped up from her seat, "Oh crap!" she said, "Noah."

And without another word she ran up the stairs, leaving Melina sitting on the couch confused. She grabbed her phone off of her dresser, where she had disobediently left it, went to her favorites list in the menu, and touched Noah's name, it rang twice, before he answered.

"Hey," she heard him say, "Somebody does know how to us a phone afterall."

"Noah, I am so sorry about yesterday," she plead. "Can I ever make it up to you?"

"Kiss my feet in front of the whole school," he said.

"Gross!" Shayna laughed, "What else do you got?"

There was silence on the other end of the phone, and then she heard Noah say, "Seriously Shayan," The tone of his voice changed to concern, "What's going on with you?"

Shayna sighed loudly in frustration, "Not you to," she said.

"Well, what do you expect? This guy shows up, and suddenly, he's taking all of your time and you're ignoring your friends." Noah didn't want to sound jealous, but he was genuinlly concerned.

"Friend," Shayna said, pointing out that he was her only one. "Noah I'm fine. Cain is an amazing person, and I promise he's not making me do anything that I don't want to do. I really enjoy spending time with him," she said reassuringly.

Shayna stayed on the phone with Noah for about an hour trying to convince him that Cain wasn't a serial killing, rapist. When they hung up she had to laugh, because she knew he was still suspicious.

Melina had left for Delany's and Shayna was alone in the house. She wanted to see Cain, but he was busy running errands for Aunt Mill in Traverse City all day. She went to her bedroom window and looked out. Sitting on the power line, across the street from her house, was a large hawk. She stared at him.

"Aiden Luca," she said his name.

She remembered what he had said. That he would "show her". If he was Cain's brother, then he would know Cain better than *anyone*. She thought.

"What secrets will you show me?" she wondered out loud.

Shayna blinked her eyes, and in an instant the massive hawk was gone. Nothing is ever going to be normal again. She realized. She moved from the window and went to her bed. She knew Aiden was the change she had sensed that morning. She sat on her bed, and wondered if it was a good or bad. Her father had trusted him to protect her, and had sent him to protect her. He was myserious and cocky, but she decided to trust him too, her father wouldn't put her in danger.

The next morning, Cain and Shayna agreed to meet in the cafeteria at lunch. When Shayna walked in, she was all that Cain saw. Everyone else in the cafeteria disappeared. Shayna couldn't help but think about what Aiden had said. He was not a creep. She thought, as she approached him. He stood up and kissed her cheek, before sitting back down with her.

"People here are bored," he said, "Aren't they?"

Shayna laughed, "You've heard rumors?"

Cain leaned towards her, "Yeah, but unfortunately, I hear what they don't say." he smiled.

Should I tell him about Aiden? Shayna asked herself, knowing that Cain could not hear what *she* didn't say. How would he react? Shayna got the impression that Aiden, for some reason, had hard feelings for Cain. She wondered if Cain felt the same way about him.

"Did you hear about Derrick?" she asked Cain.

"A little," he answered. "I was more interested in what they were saying about you." He smiled at her again, and she blushed.

"I don't even want to know," Shayna said, shaking her head.

"You're right," he laughed, "You don't. So what did *you* find out about Derrick?" Cain asked.

Shayna swallowed the bite of salad, she had been chewing on.

"He was found in the cemetary, nowhere near my father's memorial, by the grounds keeper." She gave Cain an approving smile, and noticed people were staring at them. Not letting it bother her, she continued, "The grounds keeper called the police. After the school called his parents, they sent for him to come home. Apparently they are making him go to a rehabilitation facility."

"That sounds about right," Cain said, and winked at her, "It was his idea."

"You're amazing," She squeezed his hand, and smiled. Her tranquil blue eyes sparkling.

She thought about Aiden again, and wondered if there was *anything* that he could "show" her about Cain, that could make her change the way she felt about him. Because at that moment, no one else in the world existed to her, except for Cain.

They finished lunch, and walked to advanded art, together. Shayna was thinking a lot, and was starting to piece some things together. She was certain it wasn't a coincedence that Cain had come to Interlochen.

"You took this class because of me, didn't you?" she asked him, walking through the classroom doors.

He looked at her and nodded, "I did princess," he confessed.

They had lost track of time in the cafeteria, and walked in to the Art room just as the final bell rang. They took their chairs and placed them around the still life table, as they had done the week before. Cain retaking his position behind Shayna, and to the side.

Unlike the week before, when she couldn't stop thinking about Cain, Shayna worked mostly on her drawing. She still thought about him during the class. She wondered how well he could draw, and if he even had a good view of the table from where he was, but she was able to stay more focused.

The bell rang, and Mrs. Olson told the class to turn in their drawings finished or not. After they had left the Art room, Cain kissed Shayna's neck, below her ear, before parting for their next classes. They agreed to meet at his car when school was out.

They pulled out of the school parking lot and Cain put his hand on Shayna's knee, hoping he could impel her, even if only the tiniest bit.

"So I have been hearing people talking a lot about a Winter Formal next Friday."

Shayna laughed at the thought of going to the formal, "No way!" she said.

Damn, it didn't work. Cain thought. "Why" he asked, pouting his lip out a little.

Shayna hated the thought of everyone getting all dolled up, as fake as possible, and grinding up against each other all night long. Then going off to do, God knows what, at some fancy hotel afterwards.

"Seriously? It's their foreplay," she said, talking about the other students at the art academy. "And it's my senior year, I have never been to a formal *or* prom, and I don't really plan to."

Cain laughed at her, "Well I've never been to a formal or a prom either, but I've never thought about them as foreplay," he said, still laughing, "How bout we do something else than, just you and I."

"I think I would like that better," Shayna said, touching his hand that was on her knee, and tracing his fingers, gently, with hers. She was starting to get used to his coldness.

Cain dropped Shayna off, and left to tend to his horses. He had hoped to meet Sarah, since he had missed her when he dropped Shayna off after their ride. She had gotten called into work, and wasn't home.

Shayna had not even made it in the door, when her favorite El Camino pulled up to her house.

Noah climbed out of the car and strutted up to the stoop. "Hey Shay, what do you say, what's new today?" he said, bounding up the steps, and plopping down onto the porch swing.

"You're such a dork," Shayna said. She sat down next to him and leaned her head on his shoulder, and sighed.

"You got it that bad, huh?" Noah asked.

He had never seen Shayna this way. It was like she was walking around in a daze, but she seemed more full of life than ever. Noah was worried for his friend, she barely knew this new kid.

"Mmmhmm." She did have it bad. So bad, it's good. She thought. "I wish you could get to know him."

"Why can't I?" Noah asked.

"Huh?" Shayna said, a little confused. She lifted her head off of Noah's shoulder. What did I say? She asked herself.

"You said you wished I could get to know him," Noah told her, "Why can't I"

Shayna racked her brain for something to say. She hadn't even meant to say it out loud. "I meant I *can't wait* for you to get to know him," she said, trying to convincingly shrug it off.

Noah looked at Shayna suspiciously. He sensed there was something she wasn't telling him, and if he knew Shayna, he knew that she would never tell. He would have to wait for her to slip, like she had, so he could put the pieces together.

"I can't wait either," he finally said. He saw the necklace that hung around her neck, and he reached out and touched it. "Where did you get this?"

"I found it in the attic a couple years ago," she told him. She took the stone in her hand and held it. The cold feeling reminding her of Cain, "It was my dad's."

"It's pretty cool," Noah said, "I like how the red spots look like drops of blood."

"Ironically, it's called a bloodstone," Shayna told Noah. She thought about how the bloodstone would protect her from the sun, and how powerful it truly was.

They hung out on the porch talking for a while, and then went inside to make smoothies. Noah left after his mom had called him, needing him to go to the store for her. He had gotten absolutely nowhere with Shayna regarding Cain, and was more suspicious about the two of them then before he had came to her house. Deep down inside he got an odd feeling about Cain. It wasn't a bad feeling, but it was a feeling that things weren't what they appeared.

Chapter 9

Shayna found herself walking down a dark hallway. She didn't know where she was, but she knew she was in another time period. Maybe even in another country. It was one of those things in a dream, that is never clarified, you just know.

She could feel someones hand holding her's, and she gasped in shock. She could not see who it was in the darkness, and she tried to pull her hand away, but the firm grip on the other end, only tightened They got closer to the torch burning at the end of the hallway, and her eyes focused, and she saw that it was Aiden. She was confused, but glad to see him.

"Where are we?" she asked him quietly.

Aiden gave her a mischievious smile, "I told you, I would show you, and this is the only way," he said.

He guided her to the right, down another hallway. They came to a door where they stopped. He pushed open the door, it led into a bed chamber. Shayna saw a beautiful girl, combing her hair in front of a mirror on a dark wooden dresser inside. She was Shayna's age, and was dressed in a long flowing, light blue, chamber gown. Her hair was long, and as black as Obsidions. Shayna thought she was very pretty.

The girl put the comb on the dresser, and walked toward the bed, and to Shayna's amazement, she saw Cain appear on the balcony.

"Aiden?" Shayna whispered. "Where are we?"

"That is not important," he told her, still holding her hand tightly, "Just watch."

Shayna did as he said, and looked back to the bed chamber. The girl saw Cain, and a look of surprise swept her face. Then she smiled at him, inviting him in with a wave of her hand. They sat down on the bed together and began talking.

"Why can't we hear them?" Shayna asked Aiden.

"That is not important either," he answered.

"Can they hear us?" Shayna said, and looked at him.

"No," Aiden said, and gently took her chin in his hand and turned her head back towards the bedchamber. "Watch," he insisted.

Shayna watched as the expression on Cain's face changed from, calmness, to confusion, to sadness, then to anger. He stood up and began to walk toward the balcony, then stopped.

"Her name was Roslyn," Aiden whispered, into Shayna's ear.

Shayna didn't respond. She watched silently, as Cain turned back to Roslyn, eyes red, and rushed towards her. He grabbed her, and although Shayna couldn't hear it, Roslyn clearly screamed. Shayna knew she didn't have a chance, she had felt Cain's strength herself. She watched in horror as Cain held the helpless girls hands behind her back with one hand, and with the other, he held her neck and sunk his extended canines in. Shayna was paralyzed, she didn't want to watch, but she couldn't look away. Her eyes were locked on them.

Roslyn stopped fighting Cain, and Shayna trembled as she watched him place her limp, lifeless body on the bed.

"Is she dead?" she asked Aiden. He didn't answer her. She turned her head in his direction, he was gone.

"Aiden?" She whirled around looking for him in the dark halls of the ancient castle like building she was in. Aiden was nowhere in sight. "Aiden!" she cried out again.

Shayna turned back to Roslyn's bed chamber right as Cain looked up in the direction of the doorway she was standing in. He was crying. The look on his face was remorse, and surprise. He could obviously hear something that Shayna couldn't. He was kneeling on the floor, and stood up. Quickly he ran towards the balcony, and stopped and took one last look at Roslyn lying on the bed, before he disappeared into the night. Something inside of Shayna told her to turn around and she did, just as two men and *Aiden*, ran around the corner of the hallway and right towards her. Shayna closed her eyes, and screamed. They were going to run right into her, she had nowhere to go. She braced herself for the impact. What was Aiden doing with them? She thought, and suddenly opened her eyes.

Shayna layed in bed for the rest of the night replaying the dream over, in her head. She knew that it was something that really happened. Her heart told her that. She wished she could have heard what they were saying. She wondered what had made Cain so angry, and what had made him kill Roslyn. Those questions and more ran through Shayna's mind, and she wondered, why, it was so important for her to know this part of Cain's past. But she ultimately decided that she didn't care, she knew it had happened a long time ago. At least a hundred years, and she knew that Cain had a past.

As the sun began to rise and daylight peeked through Shayna's drapes, she had came to the conclusion that she was going to accept Cain's past for what it was, and not question him on it. After all he was a *vampire*, and she figured he hadn't drank the blood of horses *all* of his life.

When Melina knocked on her door around seven thirty, there was no way Shayna was getting out of bed.

"Just get my homework for me, please," she told Melina, before she rolled over and pulled the comforter over her head.

Shayna spent the rest of the day in bed until Melina got home after school, and brought her the assignments that she missed. Shortly after Cain pulled up. Shayna was just getting out of the shower, and Melina answered the door when he knocked.

"Is Shayna home?" he asked Melina, with a voice that made her melt inside and become instantly jealous of Shayna.

"She's upstairs, I'll go get her for you."

Melina started to close the door, but Cain put his hand on it, and said, "Won't you invite me in?"

Melina wasn't about to be rude to this boy, even if she was a little jealous of Shayna.

"Of course," she said, embarassed that she didn't ask in the first place, "Please, come in," Melina opened the door wider for him, "You can have a seat in the livingroom, and she'll be right down."

Cain stepped into the foyer, "Thank you," he said.

He was not allowed into a dwelling unless invited. He smiled at Melina, and she gestured for him to go into the livingroom. She closed the door and headed up the stairs. Cain sat down on the couch, entertained by Melina's thoughts of him.

At the same time, that both Melina and Shayna appeared at the top of the stairs, Sarah walked in the front door.

"Oh, hi," Sarah said to Cain. She was a little surprised when she saw him sitting on the couch. She had been out running errands, and had not expected to return home to find an unknown boy in her livingroom.

Shayna reached the bottom of the stairs, "Mom, this is Cain. Cain this is my mom," she said, introducing the two of them.

"Sarah," Sarah said, and reached out to shake Cain's hand.

He took her hand, and she immediately felt the cold, and thought of her late husband. She looked at Shayna. Shayna knew what she had felt, and could barely hold eye contact with her mother. Sarah smiled at her daughter with raised eyebrows. Cain immediately pulled his hand away. He knew what she had felt too, and he knew what she was thinking. Although Sarah never knew for sure, she had her own theories about what her husband had been, and what Shayna is. Because Marcus Verona never verified it to her, she only had her theories.

"Nice to finally meet you, Mrs. Verona," Cain said, breaking the tension of the awkward moment that went unnoticed by Melina, who remained at the top of the stairs.

Cain searched Sarah's mind. She was a very unique individual, and she didn't care what Shayna might be. She knew her daughter was special, and Sarah wanted nothing more than for Shayna to be as happy in life, as her father was. Cain had to look away briefly. He didn't want them to see the embarassment on his face, when he felt through Sarah's mind, how much Marcus Verona had meant to this family.

"Let me get these groceries for you," Cain said, and reached down for the brown paper bags that Sarah had put on the floor when she came into the house.

"Follow Me," Shayna said, taking one of the bags out of Cain's arms.

She led him into the kitchen, and they put the bags on the cherrywood island, in the middle of the tile floor. Sarah followed them in, and started helping Shayna put the groceries away. Sarah invited Cain to stay for dinner, and he did. Although he didn't want to be impolite, he only picked at the steak she had made. Sarah had to be to the hospital early the next morning to work a double shift, so after dinner, she excused herself and went to bed.

Cain helped Shayna clean up the kitchen and do the dishes, and then they went outside and sat on the porch swing together. Shayna snuggled into Cain's side and put her arms around him. She felt so right in his arms. She looked up at him and smiled, and he kissed her forehead, and smiled back.

"Shayna I want to be this way forever," Cain said soflty, and kissed her forehead again, "Just me and you against the world Princess."

Shayna looked at him with peircing blue eyes,

"Forever," she said, and she leaned up to kiss him just as he was going to kiss her forehead again, and their lips met and the infusion took over.

What felt like electricity pulsated through their bodies, and Shayna whimpered, in ecstacy. She could kiss him forever. Every dog in the neighborhood began howling, and Shayna heard the birds, roosting in the trees, join in with their chirps and calls. Cain squeezed her harder, being careful of how fragile she was in his arms. She was his everything, he was hers. She didn't need him, he needed her.

When the neighborhood was silent again Shayna tried to pull away from Cain to look into his emerald eyes, and catch her breath. But he held her tighter and kept kissing her, gently, tenderly on her lips. Then slowly down her jawbone. The sensation felt incredible to Shayna, and she melted into his arms again. He made his way down her neck, and Shayna moaned. He kissed her neck a harder. Shayna felt his teeth, as they scraped across her tender skin. He nibbled at her, and then bit her a little, Shayna felt the sharp sting and jumped.

"Oh my God!" Cain was ashamed of himself. He sat straight up off of the swing, and Shayna fell to the porch. He immediately helped her up, and sat her back down on the swing. He knelt down in front of her, his eyes glowing more red than she had ever seen, "Oh my God!" he said again. "I am so sorry my Princess. I can't stay here, I have to go."

"No," she protested, "Please stay. I'm fine, see," she showed him her neck. There were two small red marks, that he could see under the porch light, but no blood. "You stopped. Please don't go."

"No. You stopped me," he told her, with pleading eyes. "Shayna, I love you. I have no reason to go on without you. My soul is already damned, but I won't take your life."

Shayna sighed, she knew she needed to let him go. She only had a little more than a week, and then neither one of them would ever have to be inconvenienced by the fact that he was a danger to her, again.

"Fine," she said.

"I love you," Cain told her. He kissed her below her earlobe, his favorite spot, and stood up. "You are my Princess."

She smiled up at him. He turned, and in three sprints was at his car. He opened the door to climb in, and looked back at Shayna. He hated leaving her, but hated the thought of hurting her, more.

Shayna leaned back in the swing and pulled her knees up to her chin, and watched Cain's tail lights go around the corner. She took a deep breath, finding herself smiling. After she had discovered her fate, she didn't think she would be happy after the transformation. But she knew that Cain would do anything to make the best life for her. She sat on the swing thinking about the life that she was about to begin. She was so lucky to have Cain. *He* was her dream come true.

She thought about Aiden. Why was he so persistant on showing her bad things, from Cain's past? If he was Cain's brother, why doesn't he show her good things? Why was Aiden with those men in her dream? She wondered. She had noticed that the clothes he wore when he was with them, was more the style of the time period her dream was in. When he stood with her, he wore different clothes, modern clothes.

"He must have been there," she said to herself.

It was late when Shayna finally went inside the house. She went to her room and locked her door. Opening her closet, she grabbed the screwdriver, and pried up the loose board. She took out the book, *Halfling Princess*, and sat down on her bed. She opened it, and started to read.

Chapter 10

Shayna wasn't surprised to look over and see Aiden walking next to her in the dark alley. She looked around. There were make shift shelters and shacks everywhere. She knew she was in in a large city, but she wasn't sure what time period, again.

"Please don't make me watch this again," she pled.

Aiden looked down at her, "Would you just stay away from him then?" he asked, with frustration in his voice.

"No," she told him, "Please Aiden, don't make me watch this".

"Shayna, don't you understand?" Aiden said, "He only wants your blood, and he will say anything to get it. I made a vow to protect you, and I will do anything to keep that vow."

"I don't believe that," she told him, she felt that Cain was as much in love with her, as she was with him.

They approached a little shack that had a thin stack of smoke coming from the chimney. Shayna could see candle light eminating from a small window. Aiden pulled Shayna by her hand around the small shack, and toward a window in the back.

"No Aiden," She protested.

Aiden pointed back towards the alley, "It's too late, he's coming," he said.

Shayna looked, and saw the silhouette of someone walking down the alley toward the shack. She knew it was Cain.

"You don't have to watch, but he's going to bring her outside eventually, anyway," Aiden told her, " I don't know how to wake you up. You're kinda stuck, unless you can do it yourself. I'm sorry."

Shayna glared at Aiden and turned her face away from him. She found herself looking right through the window. She saw a small fireplace and absentmindedly stepped closer to get a better look inside. The single burning candle just barely gave enough light for Shayna to see. In one corner, on the dirt floor, was a mattress with a dirty, ratty quilt on it, and in the other corner, was a table. She glanced toward the table, which held the candle, and saw a girl there, writing by the candle light. Her blonde ringlettes bouncing as she moved her pen to the ink well, dipped it in, and resumed her writing. She too, like Roslyn, looked Shayna's age and was beautiful.

Shayna turned back to Aiden, he was gone. Go figure! She thought. Shayna trusted that he meant well, but his disappearing act was getting a little irritating.

Cain approached the shack, Shayna peered through the window again, her own curiosity getting the better of her. She knew what she would probably see, and what would happen, but she didn't know why she had to look.

After the girl answered the door to Cain's knocking, the two sat down at the table together, and talked for a while. Shayna could tell that they enjoyed each other's company. Cain eventually pulled a pocket watch out of his vest pocket, and showed the girl the time. Shayna wished so much, that she could hear what they were saying.

Cain and the girl stood up, and approached one another. Shayna watched them. She couldn't take her eyes away. She felt a wave of jealousy rush through her, as Cain placed his hand on the girls neck and pulled her closer to him. She felt sick to her stomach, if that was even possible in a dream. Why is Aiden showing me *this*? She wondered. When Cain's razor sharp teeth punctured the girls skin, Shayna's jealousy grew stronger. She hated the feeling.

The girl looked like she was enjoying herself, and Cain, while he so gracefully took her blood. But, quickly the scene changed. Shayna watched as the girl grabbed Cain by the shoulders, digging her nails into his immortal flesh. She appeared to be trying to push him away from her. Cain didn't respond, he didn't even move. To Shayna he looked like he was in a trance. His eyes were closed, and aside from a little movement in his neck when he swallowed, he was virtually motionless. Shayna had never felt so helpless in her life. She was dreaming and she knew this had happened in the past, but she wished there was some way she could intervene and help the girl, and pull Cain out of the catatonic state that he was in. But, she could only watch from the window, helpless.

The blonde girl swung at Cain, trying to punch him, but he remained unphased, and she was unable to stop him. After a while she stopped fighting, and Shayna watched her body become lifeless in his arms. Tears ran down Shayna's cheeks. They felt cold to her. Everything felt so real. It was real! She remembered. Although she was assuming, she was pretty sure everything Aiden was showing her, had happened. Shayna felt sorrow for the poor girl, but mostly for Cain. When he finally pulled away from her, and saw what he had done, he fell to the dirt floor of the shack and wept over her body. She was just as beautiful in death, as she was in life. Shayna wept with Cain. She knew it was an accident, he hadn't even looked conscious.

Cain stood up, with the girl in his arms, and walked to the door. He effortlessly opened it, never loosing his hold on the girl. Shayna knew he couldn't see her, but she could see him around the side of the shack, and she crouched down with her knees to her chest, next to a small pile of fire wood. She could see Cain as he went knocking, from door to door, with the girl in his arms, with no one answering. Shayna buried her face in her knees and cried. She knew nothing could be done for the girl, she was gone.

Melina arrived at school the next morning, and immediately went to the library to meet Noah. Shayna and Cain had left before Melina, but they had not arrived at school yet. She wondered where they were. Melina sat down with Noah at a table tucked in a secluded corner.

"Morning Kiddo," Noah greeted her when she scooted her chair closer to him.

"Good morning," Melina replied.

Noah took his fedora off, and placed it in the center of the table.

"So, I can't get anything out of her," he told Melina.

"Me neither," she said, "But, I did hear her crying in her sleep last night, and I heard her yell out a name in her sleep a night or two before."

"What was the name?" Noah asked.

"Aiden, I think," Melina said, "I was listening at the door. I tried to open it, but it was locked. She never locks her door," she confessed.

Noah looked around the library. A couple other students had came in early to work on homework before classes started. Noah leaned closer to Melina, and lowered his voice. "Monday after school, she said, she wished I could get to know him," he told her.

Melina was a little dumbfounded. "So?" she said.

"Why *can't* I get to know him? I am her best friend, aren't I?" Noah explained.

"You might be on to something," said Melina, "Why *can't* you get to know him? What did you say when she said that?"

"I asked her why I couldn't, of course," he began, "And, she said, that was not what she said. She had said, "I can't *wait* for you to get to know him." Noah rolled his eyes after telling Melina what Shayna claimed to have said. "I've never felt like Shayna was lying to me before. Keeping things from me yes, but not lying to me. But I really feel like she's hiding something *and* lying about it." Noah picked his fedora up off of the table, and put it back on his head.

"Me too," Melina said. She was becoming more concerned about the situation "I do like Cain though, and I don't want to think he's a wierdo creeper, or anything."

"Well let's just stay on the down low, and we'll see what happens," Noah said. He stood up, and held his hand out to Melina, and helped her to her feet. "Don't worry kiddo," he winked at her, "We'll figure it out."

Melina couldn't believe it when she felt her cheeks burning. Noah had made her blush.

"This is kind of exciting. Trying to figure out Shayna's mystery," she winked back at him, trying to draw his attention away from her cheeks, that still burned. If he had realized that his silly pet name had made her blush, he didn't say anything, or acknowledge it. They walked out of the library, and parted ways to their classes.

When Shayna walked into the lunchroom the first thing that Cain noticed, was the high collared shirt, that had been hidden by her coat, that morning. He felt horrible for what had happened the night before, and wondered if he *should* leave for the remainder of the week, until Shayna was eighteen. Maybe it was the best thing to do. He thought. If it meant keeping Shayna safe from him, he would walk out of the lunchroom, at that very moment, and not come near her for a week. Which to Cain, was a *very*, short period of time. I should just let Aiden do, what he came here to do. He thought to himself.

Shayna sat down with him, and gave him a smile.

"Hello," she said.

"Hello, beautiful Princess," he said, greeting her.

Hearing Cain call her Princess would never grow old to Shayna, but she had something else on her mind, that she couldn't keep from him any longer.

"Cain," she said, "I need to talk to you."

She couldn't stop thinking about her dreams, and she needed answers from him.

"What is it?" he asked.

Shayna took a deep breath. Her life was getting so, crazy. "I've been having some dreams," she started.

"Okay."

"And in them, I have this guide, who is showing me these dreams." Shayna had been looking down at the floor, and looked up to make eye contact with Cain. She felt tears sting the back of her eyes, and tried to force them back. She could tell that his full attention was on her, and what she was about to say. "His name is Aiden."

Shayna's eyes never left Cain's face while she waited for a response from him.

The expression on his face reamained calm, and loving. He took her hand in his.

"Shayna, I want to tell you everything, but not here, not right now," he told her.

"Okay," Shayna said, relaxing a bit.

I'm sorry I didn't tell you before," Cain looked around the cafeteria, "I will come over, when I'm done at the shop tonight." A look of relief swept over his face. "I've been wanting to tell you," he paused briefly, "It is definitely time."

They walked to their art class together, and Cain wondered if he should tell her *everything*.

When they walked into the room, Mrs. Olson had everyone taking their original seats. That was fine with Shayna since she and Cain now sat together. She remembered that first day when he had looked at Mrs. Olson so intently, and the teacher had sent him to sit with her. Shayna wondered if Cain had impelled Mrs. Olson that day, so that he could sit next to her.

"Alright everyone," Mrs. Olson said, when the tardy bell rang, and everyone was in their seats. "If you will look to the back of the room. I have placed your still life drawings on the wall." At once, everyone turned to the back of the room. "I have written catagories on the chalk board. I would like for everyone to vote for their favorite in these catagories. I have placed a sticky note on each drawing, assigning it, it's own number."

The catagories read:
Best Lettering
Best Shading
Best use of creativeness
Best Overall

Mrs. Olson continued, "Vote for one drawing for each category. Make sure you write the number, and category, you are voting for on a piece of paper, and put them in the box I have provided," she pointed at the box, "Remember, you can vote four times, for all four catagories. You may begin."

Shayna and Cain waited for the other students to exit their seats, before getting up themselves. They walked up behind the other students, and they heard little gasps and whispers. Things like, "She's beautiful" and "Got my vote." Shayna looked at Cain, and he just shook his head and smiled, oddly at her. When the students saw Shayna approaching they stepped aside, for her to see the drawings, and immediately she saw her own face amongst them on the wall. She stepped closer, completely amazed, and grabbed for Cain's hand.

"You did this?" she asked him. He nodded his head, and just stood there and smiled at her, "It's beautiful."

He had been staring at her during class, because he had been drawing her. The drawing was incredibly perfect, it looked just like her. She was the focal point, and the still life was the background. He had captured her looking down at her own drawing, perfectly. They could hear the whispers behind them, as all the students gathered at the wall to see what the commotion was about. Cain knew this was the reaction Mrs. Olson had anticipated. He could hear the jealous thoughts of the other females in the class, regarding himself and Shayna. They envied her.

Mrs. Olson walked up behind the students, "Should we vote now?" she asked them.

"Do we need to?" A tall lanky blonde, named Jill said.

"Is everyone in consensus?" Mrs. Olson asked.

"Yes," they all said together.

Shayna couldn't help but blush. The drawing was amazing, and so was Cain.

After the class was over, Cain kissed Shayna goodbye, on the cheek.

"I'll see you tonight," he said, and turned in the other direction and disappeared down the hall. She couldn't wait for him to come to her later. She needed to hear from Cain, what Aiden was trying to say.

When school was over Shayna began walking home. She walked past the city park and noticed a familiar figure sitting on the gazebo, like he was waiting for her.

Aiden smiled at her, as she walked across the grass toward him, glaring at him the whole time. She was still upset that he had made her watch Cain, and that he had left her again.

"Hello," he said to her, when she approached him. She didn't sit down. She stood glaring at him, with her arms folded at her chest. "Will you please trust me now, and stay away from him?"

"Aiden, I stayed and watched, he didn't mean to kill her, and he was upset and tried to get her help," she told him, defending Cain. She knew Cain wouldn't hurt her. He tried so hard, not to, "Besides, I told him about you, and he's going to tell me everything tonight."

"We'll see if he tells you *everything*. But, Fine," Aiden said, and stood up and walked over to her, "I just want to make sure he doesn't hurt you, and I know he will. He can't resist, and if he kills you, then I don't succeed in what I came here to accomplish," he walked to the other side of the gazebo.

"What *did* you come here to accomplish Aiden?" Shayna asked him.

"To make sure he doesn't have *you* too!" he exclaimed.

"Doesn't it matter to you, that I want him too?" she asked. She didn't care that Cain had taken lives, she didn't care about his past, she loved him.

"You won't," Aiden said, then paused, "When you know."

All Shayna saw next was a brilliant flash of light, and feathers falling to the boarded platform of the gazebo. She ran to where Aiden had been standing, and looked up expecting to see him flying away, but he was gone. She wondered what he had in store to "show her" next.

"I'll never stop loving him!" she yelled into the air. She believed Aiden meant well, but he just didn't seem to understand. Hadn't he ever been in love before? She wondered.

When Shayna walked up to her house, Melina was walking out the front door, leaving for work at the Dutch Cup, but she stopped to talk to her sister.

"Hey Shay," she said, "What's new?"

"Not too much," Shayna answered. She had noticed that Melina had seemed more interested in her these days. She knew it was probably because of Cain. "What time do you work until?" she asked Melina.

"Ten thirty," Melina said, then changed the subject, "So, are you and Cain going to the Winter Formal?"

Shayna laughed, "What do you think?"

"I think," she looked at Shayna, in a matter of fact way, as she opened the door to the Honda Prelude, "That you two, would have fun, and should go."

"Maybe we would, but, I still don't want to go," Shayna stated.

"Whatever!" Melina said, but she wasn't about to give up, "Come on Shay. Do it for me," she paused and looked at her twin with pleading eyes, "Do it for yourself. High School is almost over, ya know? You should go to at least one dance, before you lose the opportunity," Melina got in the car, started it up, and pulled away from the house, Shayna stood at the curb watching the Prelude disappear.

Maybe Melina is right, she thought. Maybe I should attend one formal function before we're out school.

Shayna laughed, "Yeah right," she said out loud, "Maybe senior prom." She turned and walked inside the house.

Chapter 11

Cain never showed up like had said he would, and didn't answer his phone when Shayna called him either. She figured that whatever had kept him away, must have been important.

She went to bed around eleven o'clock dreading what dreams may come to her. When she finally did drift into oblivion, she found herself in the meadow, surrounded by daisies, and standing face to face with Aiden.

"Now what?" she said to him, rolling her eyes.

He chuckled, "Nothing tonight Shayna," he said, and reached for her hand, and lead her to the downed tree to sit down. "Tonight I talk."

"What if I don't want to listen?" she asked, she *didn't* want to listen to him.

"That's fine," he said, smiling at her, "If you can wake yourself up, you don't have to listen."

He won that battle, Shayna could never wake herself up out of a dream.

"What do you want then?" she demanded.

"Shayna, those girls I showed you weren't just random girls," he told her looking into her eyes. "They were Halflings, like you." He wanted her to understand exactly what he was trying to tell her about Cain, and why he was there.

It took a moment for what Aiden was saying to sink in. When it finally did, a lot of things began to come clear to Shayna.

"He's a Changeling," she said quietly.

Aiden nodded his head, "Yes. He killed those girls, before they ever had a chance to turn. You saw what he did to Roslyn, and that poor girl in Amsterdam," he looked angry when he spoke Roslyn's name, "Roslyn had agreed to change him, but then changed her mind. He took her blood, and her life," he said, and sat down next to Shayna on the tree. "The poor girl had agreed to change him too, she never had a chance." Aiden looked away into the distance, picking at the bark on the tree, and gouging a divet in it with his finger nail.

"I don't think he has any control, once he tastes the blood," Shayna told him, "He can't help himself, believe me Aiden. I've processed this through my mind many times. I saw him," she said, thinking back to what she had seen, "He didn't mean to kill those girls."

"Shayna you're delusional!" Aiden said to her, "He's using you to get what he wants," he stood back up and began pacing. "He wants your blood, and if you're not careful, he *will* kill you. Whether he means to or not."

"I'm delusional?" she asked, and laughed at him, "*You're* the one invading my dreams."

"I'm just trying to make sure you don't die in his hands. You're no good to me dead. You're father sent me to protect you from Changelings like Cain. I swore when I set out to spread his ashes over Humboldt Bay, that I would never let Cain, or any other Changeling touch you," he said, and he had every intention of keeping that promise. He kicked at the ground, and looked at Shayna like he was embarassed, and said, "I have to be honest with you Shayna. Entering your dreams for the last few years, has been nothing compared to actually standing face to face with you, and inhaling you." Shayna blushed and Aiden continued, "If I would have known how truly magnificent you are, I would have tried harder to find you, and come a lot sooner," he knelt down in front of her, on one knee, took her hand, and said, "For myself."

"Aiden," she said to him, "I do love Cain." Although she was flattered, she knew Cain was her soul mate.

Aiden stood up, clearly frustrated, "Fine Shayna. See it your way," he said, "But, I will show you how uncontrolably lethal he really is."

"Aiden please. Why is this so hard for *you* to understand?" Shayna said, "Can't you trust *me*?"

"I don't trust him, Shayna," Aiden spat out. He turned around and walked into the meadow, "I'll show you Shayna. You will believe me!"

Shayna watched Aiden walk across the meadow, and out of sight. She didn't try to stop him because she knew, neither one of them were about to budge on the way they felt about Cain. It would just lead to another pointless argument, ending in Aiden promising to "show her". She took a deep breath, in anticipation of what he could possibly show her this time, that would make her change her mind about Cain.

She was beginning to miss the old dreams of Aiden. When he wasn't trying to stop her from loving, who she believed, was her soul mate. But, Shayna's convictions were strong and pure. Aiden would have to try harder, and Shayna had a feeling he would.

Shayna waited for Cain, for twenty minutes after Melina had left the house, and finally gave up and made her way to school. She wondered where he was, and she hoped and prayed, that he had not left for the rest of her mortal existence. She hoped he was already at the academy, but he was not. He didn't show up later either, and still didn't answer Shayna's calls or texts. By the end of the day, Shayna had no other choice, but to believe that he was gone.

On her way home from school she stopped at 'Between the Lines', to talk to Aunt Mill. She did feel a little better when she left the bookstore, with the reassurance from Aunt Mill, that Cain was fine, and although she didn't know where he was, he would be back soon. The seemingly old woman said she didn't sense or see, anything out of the ordinary.

By the time Shayna laid down to go to bed, she had still not heard from Cain. She slept dreamless, but woke up often, sweating and trembling.

When morning came, she was getting dressed and stopped and looked at herself in the bathroom mirror.

"One more week," she said to the reflection, "Then the big day."

She had decided she wasn't going to wait too long for Cain, and after waiting long enough, she grabbed her backpack, and headed for the door. She opened it, and to her surprise, there stood Cain leaning against the passenger door of his car, waiting for her. She smiled, and all but ran to him, wrapping her arms around his neck.

"Don't ever do that to me again," she scolded. "I thought you were gone, and that I would be alone for the next week."

He took her face in his hands, and kissed it all over, careful not to touch her lips with his.

"I'm sorry Princess," he said. "I had to go take care of some things at the last minute. It won't happen again," he promised.

Shayna stood on her tip toes, and tried to kiss him. He gently put his finger on her lips and stopped her.

"Not now, we have to go to school, and people might see us."

"Okay," she whispered to him, "I'm just glad you're here."

He opened the car door for her and she sat down on, the already warm, leather seat. He closed the door and walked around to the other side, and climbed in himself.

Cain pulled into the school, and parked. He looked at Shayna and smiled. His green eyes sparkling, with what looked to Shayna like excitement.

"I have a surprise for you," he said.

"You do?" she asked, curiously.

They climbed out of the car, and walked to the front of it, reaching for each other's hands.

"I do," he said, still smiling, "But it all depends on what your mom says."

Shayna wasn't used to any of this. Cain was the first boyfriend she had ever had, and she wasn't even quite sure, if that was what he was. She was pretty sure he was *more* than her boyfriend. She wasn't used to surprises either, although she had gotten the surprise of her life, the day in the attic, when she had found her father's things, that he had hidden there for her.

"I can't meet you at lunch today, Princess. I have to run to the bookstore, and keep shop, while Aunt Mill goes to an appointment she has," Cain said to Shayna, when they walked into one of the various school buildings. He kissed her forehead, wishing he could just . kiss her sweet lips, and savor the taste for the rest of the day. "But, meet me at my car after school, and we'll go talk to your mom." He gave her his best, most handsome smile, and pulled away from her, leaving her standing in the hallway, with the other students shuffling in around her.

Shayna barely made it through the day with the anxiety, of what Cain's surprise was, taking over. The final bell rang at the end of the day and she didn't even stop to get the books that she needed, for the weekend, out of her locker. I know the assignments, and have the internet. She told herself, justifying her decision.

Cain was right where she knew he would be when she exited the Drama building, at the front passenger door of his car, waiting to open it for her.

He kissed her on the cheek, and whispered, "I missed you my Princess," in her ear, before she sat down on the leather seat of the BMW.

Shayna was anxious and curious to find out what he had planned. He *had* been able to surprise her with the hot spring. He had been right about that. As far as she knew, no one knew it was there. But what could this be? She wondered.

"Are you excited?" he asked her, climbing into the car on the driver side.

"I have to admit, that I am," Shayna said, "I don't have a clue what it could be."

"Don't worry," he told her with confidence, and putting his hand on her knee, "You're going to love it."

Cain started the car, and left the school. When they walked up to Shayna's front door, Cain opened the door, and motioned for Shayna to walk in first.

"Go get your mom," he whispered, when she walked in past him.

"Mom!" Shayna yelled into the house, she knew her mother was awake, "Can you come down here please?"

"You didn't have to yell," Cain said to her.

"Yes I did," Shayna said sarcastically, and smiled.

Sarah appeared at the top of the stairs, a little surprised to see Shayna *and* Cain.

"What is it Shay? I'm getting ready for work," she said, descending the stairs.

"Um, Cain has something he wants to ask you," she told Sarah when she reached the bottom of the stairs, she guided her to sit down on the couch, in the livingroom. Shayna sat down next to her, and Cain took a seat in the chair across from them.

"What is it Cain?" Sarah asked, now almost as curious as Shayna, who also, was hearing this for the first time.

"Well Mrs.Verona, I know Shayna's birthday is next weekend," Cain began. He made eye contact with Sarah, and continued to hold it, so that his connection to her would be stronger, "And I have planned something very special for her," Cain glanced briefly at Shayna, "If, you allow her to go, that is."

Cain waited for any sort of response from Sarah, whether it be mental, or physical. His eyes lit up noticably, when he heard her think, before she said,

"And, where are you planning on taking my daughter, Cain?"

Cain had not fully impelled her mind, because, although he wanted Shayna to go with him, he also wanted it to be more Sarah's decision than his own. He just gave her mind, a sort of push, towards saying yes.

"Well," he said looking at Shayna, knowing she had been waiting all day for this moment, "I have theater tickets, and would also like to take her to dinner tonight."

"That doesn't sound so bad," Sarah said, easing up a little.

"On Mackinac Island," Cain added.

Shayna eyes sparkled in delight, and a smile formed on her face. Cain would give the world to see her smile like that everyday.

"You would be gone all night?" Sarah asked Cain, realizing what he was getting at, and ruining the joy of Shayna's moment.

Mackinac Island, was a couple hours away, Shayna realized. Her excitement began to grow again.

"Yes ma'am," Cain answered, "But if it's any consolation, we would be more than happy to take Melina, and the girls would have their own room."

Cain really didn't care if Melina came along. He had gotten an extra ticket just in case. He only wanted to make Shayna happy. He had nothing but the utmost respect for Shayna, and didn't want her mom to think he was trying anything sneaky.

Both Cain and Shayna sat anxiously, waiting for an answer from Sarah. Cain wondering if she would ask any of the questions, he knew she was thinking. When he finally heard her mental response, he made eye contact with Shayna, and nodded his head, pleased that her mother approved.

"Cain, I don't think it will be necessary to take Melina along with you," Sarah smiled at them both. "I don't know you yet, young man, but I trust my daughters judgement. I want you guys to have a wonderful time."

Cain was satisfied that he had not let his power over Sarah influence her decision, to let Shayna go, too much. She truly was comfortable letting Shayna go with him.

"Really Mom?" Shayna was ecstatic. She couldn't believe, that her mother was letting her go away for the night with Cain.

Sarah almost couldn't believe it either, but she also knew, that they belonged together. Who was she to stop it, and Shayna would be an adult soon.

She looked at her daughter with eyes full of love, "Have fun Shay, but," she gave Cain and Shayna a stern look, "Shayna *will* have her own room."

"Yes ma'am," Cain didn't hesitate to say, "Of course."

Shayna hugged her mom, and kissed her on the cheek twice.

"Thanks Mom. I love you." She jumped up and went to Cain, hugging him too. She wanted to kiss him on the mouth, but knew she couldn't. So she hugged him tighter, and whispered in his ear, "I can't wait. I love you."

While Shayna packed an over night bag for the trip, Cain remained downstairs with Sarah. Supplying her with the name of the hotel, which he had not told Shayna, the phone number, and the room numbers. She also had requested his driver's license number, and his license plate number. Cain found it all a little comical, but gave everything to her, without question. Promising to have Shayna home Saturday afternoon.

They were able to finally get out of Interlochen, after filling up the BMW's gas tank at the EZ mart, around four thirty. Sarah had kissed her daughter goodbye, brushing her hair off of her shoulder.

"Have a wonderful time Shayna," she had said. She felt like she was to letting her daughter go for good.

Shayna was nervous about the evening. She felt one hundred percent safe with Cain, and wasn't going to let anything that Aiden had said ruin her night. The last two weeks with Cain, had been incredible to Shayna. Although everything was all very new and a little weird to her, she had developed unusually strong feelings for Cain. She felt like she had known him forever.

It would take them around two and a half hours to get to Mackinaw City, where they would have to get on a ferry to the island, where no cars were allowed. They would have to drive north along the coast of Lake Michigan, to the tip of the Lower Peninsula. Shayna sat pondering on whether she should bring up Cain's secret, or let him.

They had been on the road for about an hour, when Shayna looked at him, and said, "Cain," Now or never. She thought. "Why didn't you tell me, that you are a Changeling?"

Cain was silent for a while. Shayna turned and looked out the window, into the dark northern Michigan country side, not sure what the silence meant.

Finally, Cain sighed. "Shayna, my past is the worst thing that I must exist with everyday," he said, and zipped around a corner a little faster than Shayna would have liked. "Roslyn was the one who found me in the alley that fateful night. She told me that she had thought I was too beautiful to leave this earth, so she took me home to her father. I remember he cut his wrist, with a dagger, and fed me his blood," Cain winced at the thought of his change.

Shayna could tell that Cain did not like talking about the night he should have died. The only other person, he had ever spoke to about it was Aunt Mill.

Cain continued in a soft whispered voice, that Shayna had to strain to hear. "Because most of my blood was already gone when she found me, and it couldn't be returned to me. I turned into a Changeling. An existance no vampire wants."

Shayna was sure that the feeling that she felt inside at that moment was pretty similar to the one Cain had, when he recovered from his transformation, and found out what he had become.

"That was selfish of Roslyn," she said quietly.

Cain looked at Shayna. She never ceased to amaze him.

"That is exactly how I felt that night. She *had* been selfish. I told you I wished I had died that night," he said.

He accelerated the BMW faster, and they raced along next to the Lake Michigan. Shayna knew Cain would never let anything happen to them, but she became nervous when she felt like at any moment, they would leave the safety of the road and sail into the glistening water.

Cain went on, "She made a deal with me. She didn't want to be a vampire, and she wanted to actually die before she turned."

Shayna's full attention was on Cain. She knew what it was like, to not have a choice, about who you would be, and what you would be.

"She was only sixteen when she found me," Cain told Shayna, "So she told me to return to her the night before her eighteenth birthday, and she would complete my change. And then I, was to take her life. I agreed." It was getting dark out, Cain appeared to close his eyes briefly and sigh before he continued, "So I left my home for two years, and I came back the night before her eighteenth birthday. When I came to her bed chamber, she told me she could not fulfill her end of the deal. She had found somebody she loved, and wanted to spend the rest of eternity with him."

Shayna spoke up before he could go on, " Couldn't she have still changed you?"

"Yes. She could have. But she refused. She had promised her lover that she would never share her blood with another, and she meant to stand by her promise. I understood, and I got up to leave, but I kept thinking that, she should have left me behind the stables that night. I didn't know what to do, or where I was going. I was so angry. I just had to get out of there."

Cain reached for the gear shift, and Shayna placed her hand on his and said.

"But you didn't."

"No," Cain said quietly, "I didn't. My mind filled with absolute rage, and I was blinded. Everything happened so fast. I only meant to make her change me. I didn't know if I would have another chance." Cain shifted the car. The engine purred. "I had spent the whole time I was away, researching what I was, and what she was. I knew the existance of a Halfling Princess was rare," Cain closed his eyes again, it was draining to remember.

Shayna looked up, and almost screamed when she saw nothing but water in front of them in the dimming daylight. Cain opened his eyes, and the car followed the road around the bend, without crossing a single line.

"Shayna," he spoke again, "The moment I tasted her blood my world was over." He looked and Shayna with intensely sad eyes, "I never meant to kill her, I couldn't stop. I tried."

Confirmation obtained. Shayna knew he hadn't meant to kill the girls in her dream. She had seen what had happened, but now there was a new question burning on her mind.

"Why did you come to Michigan Cain?" she asked, unsure if she really wanted the answer.

Cain's lips parted a little, and Shayna new he hated telling her.

"I came for you. But, I never thought in all eternity, that I would end up having the feelings that I have for

you. I could never bring myself to drink your blood."
He needed her to understand him, that he loved her. He
needed her to trust him. He took her hand, and squeezed
it, "I don't want to change, if it means I get to keep you
for the rest of my existance."

Shayna took in a deep breath, "Which isn't as long
as *my* existance would be," she said. She had read in the
Halfling book, that Changelings only have around five
hundred years to have a Halfling Princess change them,
or they would truly die forever. From what Shayna
could gather, Cain only had about two hundred left. "I
love you, Cain," she told him, "I have never thought
that you would hurt me. I just wish that you would have
been the one to tell me. Not some hawk on a power trip,
trying to save me from myself." She smiled at him, she
understood.

"I think Aiden means well," Cain said, "He just
hates me."

"Why?" Shayna asked, she had meant to ask
Aiden, but he always took off before she got the
chance.

"I haven't been able to figure that one out, yet. He's
really good at blocking me out of that part of his mind,"
Cain himself, wished he knew why his younger brother
hated him so. "Shayna I mean what I said, I will stay a
Changeling for you. I don't want your blood for my
own selfish reasons. I want your own transformation, to
not be tainted by the presence of my blood in your
body." The BMW suddenly came to a stop, and Cain
took both of Shayna's hands in his, and looked deep
into her eyes, "I mean this Princess, I love you and I
will forever more, exist for *you.*"

Shayna looked at him with passion in her eyes, and
promised, "And I for you Cain. I don't care about your
past, I just want you in my future."

He squeezed her hands, before pulling his away, and putting the car in gear. He started driving again.

"I would kiss you right now, but we have to move. There is a truck carrying fuel about a mile behind us," he didn't want their kiss to kill them. They were both vulnerable to death, in their current forms.

Shayna knew, and agreed, "Yeah, no kiss now."

They stepped off of the ferry a little before seven o'clock. Shayna breathed in the smells of the island. Warm and sweet, and filled with the aroma of chocolate fudge. The island had remained partialy open to the public for the season, due to the lack of snow, and the unusually warm winter. Her father had brought her family to the island once when she was younger, but she hadn't returned since. Cain found them a horse drawn buggy. The horse was all decked out in the most grand black and silver harnesses. The buggy looked like it was fit for royalty. He helped Shayna climb inside, and paid the driver. He didn't need to give the driver directions. The buggy, unbeknownst to Shayna, belonged to the hotel they were going to stay at. The Grand Hotel.

Cain climbed into the buggy, and sat beside Shayna.

"We'll get to the hotel faster this way," he told her, taking her hand and putting it in his lap, "We kind of need to hurry. After seven thirty, no street clothes. The hotel requires formal evening attire only."

"Wait what?" Shayna said, mimicking Noah, "Are we staying at the Grand Hotel?"

Cain nodded his head, with a smile on his face.

"Cain you told me to bring something to sleep in and something to wear home." Shayna was embarassed, "You never metioned formal anything."

Cain just smiled, and remained silent.

Shayna couldn't believe she was going to stay at the Grand Hotel. She had always wanted to, but thought it would be something that came when she was older. She loved Mackinac Island. She loved everything about it. The horses, the fudge, the lilacs. The old fashioned Victorian style of the whole island. She had always dreamed of someday owning a cottage on the island. When she had come when she was little, she had fallen in love with the romanticism of the place. She read every book she could get her hands on, and knew quite a bit of the history of the island.

The hotel came into view and Shayna was speechless. The large three story white Victorian *palace* sparkled with little twinkling white lights. It was more beautiful than she remembered.

The buggy stopped in front of the entrance to the hotel, and Shayna asked Cain as he helped her out, "So am I just supposed to stay in my room for the rest of the evening, or what?"

They walked through two large doors into a foyer, and Cain pulled her close to him.

"Don't worry Princess. I left something in your room, for you to wear."

Shayna was confused, "What do you mean, *you* left something in my room?" she questioned, "You were here? When?"

"Yesterday," he admitted. "I wanted this to be perfect for you."

Shayna smiled, "What if my mom had said no?" she asked.

"Then, I would have given her an extra little push," he said smiling, and opened another door for her.

They entered the lobby of the hotel, and Shayna felt like she had stepped into a whole different era in time. Everything was so elegant, there was crystal, and vevlet everywhere that she looked. She looked up at Cain proudly looking down at her and she wrapped her arms around his neck, like she had done earlier in the morning, at her house. He returned the embrace, and she whispered into his ear, while standing on her tip toes.

"You're amazing."

They checked in, and Cain rushed them up stairs to change. Dinner was at eight o'clock, and they were already pressed for time.

He unlocked the door to Shayna's room, handed her the key card, and said, "Everything you'll need, is inside. I'm right next door if you need me." He kissed her cheek goodbye, and she looked at him nervously, "Go," he urged, turning her around toward the room, and giving her a gentle push further inside, "I love you," he said.

Shayna turned to face him, and he was gone. It must run in the family. She thought. She shut the door and turned back around to view the room. It was as elegant as the lobby. There were white roses all over the room, in crystal vases. The room was the size, and style of a studio apartment. There was a living room area, with plush white furniture and a huge white lace covered canopy bed, with a white velvet comforter covering it. The white roses were complemented by a vase sitting on the coffee table, with a single red rose in it. Shayna could see a card attatched to the rose and walked over to the table.

My Princess,
These roses don't even compare
To how pure your beauty is.
Meet me in the lobby at 7:50

~ 144 ~

Eternally yours,
Cain.
P.S. *Your dress is on the bed*

Shayna picked up the vase and smelled the red rose as she walked over to the bed. The scent was so sweet. It reminded her of her mothers perfume.

On the bed was a white polyester garment bag. She put the rose on the bedside table and carefully unzipped the bag, and folded the sides back. When the dress was exposed, and Shayna saw it, she felt a chill run up her spine. It looked exactly like the one she wore in her dream in the meadow.

She pulled it out of the bag, and examined it. It was exactly the same, all the way down to the silver trimmed edges. She actually had to pinch herself. She was beginning to think that, maybe, everything was truly a dream. She walked over to the full length mirror hanging on the bathroom door, and held the dress up to her body. It was so beautiful. She placed the dress back on the bed, and began to undress.

Shayna didn't need to do anything to herself, besides put the dress on. She had found a pair of sparkling silver slippers under the dress bag when the bag had slipped off the bed and fallen to the floor. If she hadn't found them, she had been prepared to wear her boots. The dress flowed elegantly to the floor, and would have hidden them from view.

She gave herself one last look in the mirror, amazed at how she looked in the dress, and went out the door to the hall way. She approached the elevator, and noticed it was still on the first floor when she reached for the call button. She turned and headed for the stairs instead. She didn't want to keep her prince waiting.

Cain couldn't hear Shayna's thoughts, but he knew she was coming by the thoughts of the other hotel guests, when she came into their vision. Their minds were focused on the grand staircase. Cain turned and looked to the top of the stairs. Shayna was walking down, eyes focused on him. It felt like the world around them had stopped. He couldn't believe the beauty, that a single girl held.

Her hair, as usual, was pulled back halfway and the rest of her chocolate curls fell loosely over her shoulders. He didn't take his eyes off of her as she made her decsent down the stairs.

He met her at the bottom, offering her his hand when she was about to take the final step down. "You look stunning Princess," he told her, and kissed her hand.

Shayna blushed, mainly because she *knew* she looked stunning. She had never seen herself look more amazing.

In all of Cain's existance he had never met a woman, that he looked at, the same way he looked at Shayna, or that he felt about, the same way he felt about Shayna. He would die for her. He would kill for her. He would do anything she wanted. He would give her anything she wanted. He was *hers!*

"Where did you get this dress?" Shayna asked him.

"It is Aunt Mill's," he said examining her, himself. He couldn't get over how stunning she truly was in it.

"So where are we going, good sir?" she asked Cain curiously, with the most beautiful smile he had ever seen.

"Well," he said, leading her past the reception desk, "We're not actually going anywhere. Everything that I have planned for the night, is all right here at the hotel."

"I didn't know the hotel has a theater," she said falling, more in love with the place every second.

"It's more like an opera house," Cain said.

With eyes huge, and reflecting every chandelier crystal in the hotel, she looked at him, "Opera house? Are you serious?"

Cain smiled in silence, pleased with himself, and lead her in to the Main Dining Room.

With her binocculars on her lap, Shayna sat on the balcony staring out at the stage. The opera was over, but she remained silently in her seat, in a state of awe. She had never experienced anything like it. So heart touching, and moving, although she could not understand what they were saying. It made her want to learn more about her Italian background.

Cain touched her knee, and she jumped. He felt bad disturbing her. But they were the only two remaining, "Shall we?" he asked quielty.

"Of course," she said, and stood up, "I kind of spaced off. I'm sorry."

He smiled.

They exited the balcony together. Shayna couldn't believe the hotel had an opera house hidden inside of it. They walked down an empty corridor towards the stairs.

"Do you know what time it is?" Shayna asked him.

Cain pulled a very old looking, but shiny, gold pocket watch out of the pocket of the absloutley amazing looking black tuxedo that he wore. She recognized the watch from her dream, but did not say anything.

"It's eleven fifteen," he said her, "Why? Are you tired?"

"No," she told him, "I'm wide awake. That's why I asked. I'm not ready to go to sleep yet."

Cain had an idea, "Let's go for a walk," he said.

They reached the bottom of the stairs, and Cain pulled her towards the emergancy exit, and pushed open the door. She didn't have time to protest, but she wouldn't have anyway. They came out on the side of the hotel, on the beach. The night was cold, and Cain immediately took off his coat, and put it over Shayna's shoulders.

The moon cast a bright glow over the beach and they could see the waves, of lake Huron, crashing on the shore in the clear night.

"This night couldn't be more perfect," she said to him.

They stepped on to the sand, and walked towards the water. Cain wrapped his arms around her. She was so small and petite. She almost disappeared his his arms. He wanted to keep her nestled in his arms, and hold her forever.

"We can come back here anytime you want to Princess," Cain said, "This place is one of my favorite places in the world. I love it here."

They walked as far as they could down the beach talking, and holding hands. When they turned back they could see The Grand Hotel sparkling, like a small city, in the distance.

"Cain?" Shayna said quielty, "I've been thinking about something, that I need to talk to you about, all night."

Cain stopped walking and looked down at her, "What is it Princess?"

The breeze off of the lake was blowing his own shoulder length locks, all about, in a way that Shayna thought made him even more attractive, than ever. She knew she was making the right decision.

"I want to change you."

"No," he said abruptly, "I can't, I won't let you!" He started walking again.

Shayna grabbed his hand and pulled him back to her. She looked into his eyes, pleading with her own.

"Cain, I've been thinking this through." His eyes reflected the moon like emeralds, making him irristable, "I don't want to live forever, without you," she told him.

"Shayna, I don't want to kill you," he said.

He knew the he would never be able to stop himself, from drinking all of *her* sweet blood.

"No," she said.

Shayna hadn't been accepted into NYU, on a full scholarship for just her artistic abilities. She was a very intellegant, and determined young woman, with a 4.0 GPA. While she had been watching the opera, and falling in love with it, she was also thinking of ways to keep Cain with her forever.

"I know what to do. I have to take your blood first. That's the only way to do it," she said eagerly, "I know it will be fine. It will work," she pled with him, "Please Cain."

Three hundred years, two dead Halfling Princesses, and two near misses that had been spoiled by Aiden, and Cain couldn't believe that he had never thought of taking *their* blood first. What a fool I am! He thought. She *is* amazing!

But he still had to say, "No Shayna, your blood is special. Mine will ruin it. You are different than other Halfling Princesses. Your blood is very powerful. Your father was a special kind of vampire, he was a 'Born' vampire."

Cain began to walk down the beach toward the hotel again. Shayna quickly followed after him.

"Cain wait!" she cried. She was not going to give up, even if it meant attacking him herself, and taking his blood on the fateful night, that was soon approaching, "I don't care! Don't you understand? You can't ever leave me, and if we don't do this, you will."

He stopped again and faced her, "Shayna..."

"Stop Cain!" she said forcefully. He was going to hear her out. "You keep telling me, how you would feel if something happened to me. Haven't you ever thought about how I would feel, if something happened to *you*? Don't you think about how I feel knowing, I have a limited amount of time with you?" She hated sounding selfish, but she pled her case anyway, "I can prevent it, I can save you," she felt a sharp pain deep inside her chest, "Cain, please."

Cain was speechless. He couldn't do anything but stare at her. He didn't know what she was thinking, but he could see the pain in her eyes, when she spoke of loosing him. She *had* thought it all out. How could he tell her "no", when she felt so passionately about it. He felt selfish for only thinking about how *he* felt.

He suddenly grabbed her and pressed his lips hard to hers. If he had been hoping for the euphoric feeling they both shared with their kiss, he hadn't been disappointed. It took over as soon as their lips touched. He picked her up off of the sand with one arm under her legs so that the waves, that instantaineously began lapping at their feet, wouldn't get her dress wet. He held her in his arms kissing her, feeling her tounge inside of his mouth and taking in her sweet, fruit like taste.

Shayna didn't have a doubt in her mind that he was agreeing to the change. She kissed him harder, to show her gratitude. The waves continued to splash at Cain's feet, and they remained in their embrace kissing long after the sensation of ecstacy was over. When they finally ended the kiss, Cain carried Shayna back to the hotel.

She was asleep when then finally arrived and he had to have the concierge open her door for him, because he couldn't find her key. He wasn't about to disrespect her body, and search for it, and, she was sleeping too peacefully to wake. He stepped inside the room, and pushed the door shut with his foot. He walked her to the bed, and pulled back the velvet comforter, and layed her down. He gently pulled the sliver slippers she wore off her feet, and stood back, and looked at her. He smiled to himself when he thought of being with such a perfect creature, forever.

He leaned over her, and kissed her forehead.

"Goodnight Princess," he said, and pulled the comforter over her. He dimmed the lights down and quietly left the room.

Cain had controlled his instincts very well through out the evening, but he was getting hungry. The smell of blood, everywhere he turned, was taking control. He walked past his own room, toward the grand staircase. It was time to hunt.

Chapter 12

Shayna had to remind herself where she was when she woke up. She remembered being on the beach, but not coming back to the hotel. She realized she must have fallen asleep, somewhere in between. How she got into her room puzzled her. She felt her bra, and tucked safely inside, was her room key. Cain must have brought me in. She thought. But, how?

She sat up in the plush bed, still dressed in Aunt Mill's gown. The balcony doors were open slighlty, and there was a soft breeze enetering the room. The fresh morning air smelled so good to Shayna.

She got out of the bed and walked to the french doors, leading to the balcony. She opened them all the way and to her surprise Cain was standing there, leaning against the balcony rail, looking out at the lake. Shayna realized then, that their rooms shared the balcony. He turned with a jolt towards her, when he heard the doors open, but instantly smiled as their eyes met.

"Good morning," he said. She looked exactly the same as she had, when he had laid her in the bed. Stunning.

Her scent filled his nostrils, mixed with the cold winter air, it was the sweetest thing he had ever smelled. His throat burned. He was beginning to crave the unique burn that came only from the scent of her sweet blood. He was getting better at controlling his urges to drink it, to taste it.

"Morning," Shayna said, and stepped out of the room onto the balcony.

He took her in his arms, inhaling more of her. "Are you sure about this Shayna?" he asked.

"I've never been so sure about anything in my life." She squezzed him harder. "I want this."

Cain ran his fingers through her hair. "I love you Shayna, like I've never loved before, and I will forever treat you like the princess that you are," he said, kissing her softly on her neck, careful not to let himself taste her sweet skin. "We should go down stairs, before breakfast is over."

"Actually, I'm not all that hungry right now," Shayna repsponded. "I am still full from dinner."

"Okay," he said.

They didn't need to check out for another two hours, and Cain wasn't ready to take Shayna off of the island yet. Before he could suggest going for another walk, Shayna said, "Can we go down to the beach, now that it's daylight. I would like to see it again."

"Sounds great," Cain replied, he was glad she wanted the same thing.

Cain had left the island during the night, and had hunted until just before the sun came up. He took down a large cow of an elk, just north of Atlanta, Michigan. The elk hadn't been as satisfying, as one of his champion bloodline horses, but it would hold him over until he returned home.

Shayna gestured to herself, "I'm going to go freshen up a bit," she said.

He lifted her chin gently, examining her face, "You are so beautiful just the way you are. You don't need to freshen anything." He kissed her neck softly.

"I'm going to go change," she said and smiled, "I've been wearing this dress since last night."

"Okay," he said, "Go."

Shayna wanted to kiss him. She wished it was that simple. She wondered what their kiss would be like after their transformations. Would it change? Her heart raced in anticipation, and she pulled away from him, and backed up towards the room.

"I'll be right back," she said.

"I'll wait for you here."

He wanted more than just a brief kiss on the neck, or on the cheek. He wanted to scoop her up in his arms, and take her into her room, and lay her down on the white velvet bed, and kiss her all day. He wanted to stay in that room with her forever.

Cain stepped forward to follow her in, he needed more, he wanted to taste her sweet lips, to caress her body. But he stopped himself as she shut the door. He couldn't. He wasn't sure if he would be able to control himself, if it went too far. He let the door close. Wishing he could trust himself more, but, knowing not going into the hotel room with her, was the best thing.

After spending the morning walking along the lakeshore, and picking up unique rocks along the way, they headed back to the hotel to get their things and head to the ferry dock. Shayna had traded in Aunt Mill's dress, for a pair of khaki colored cordaroy pants, and a white hooded sweatshirt.

Shayna never wanted to leave, she would stay on the island forever if she could. She loved every aspect of it. She planned on holding Cain to his promise, of bringing her back whenever she wanted.

The drive home went by too fast for Shayna. She didn't want to be away from Cain, and dreaded him dropping her off at home. They talked a lot about how everything would happen on the fateful day. They decided to come back to the island, to consummate their arraingement, and stay until they had both fully recovered from their very different changes.

Shayna was scared and excited at the same time. She was almost a little aroused even. Neither one of them knew exactly what would transpire. Shayna always had planned on maintaining her innocence until she was married, but to complete Cain's transformation, she would have to give herself to him. And she was ready to. She would be his forever anyway, the didn't need a piece of paper to document that fate.

They pulled up in front of Shayna's house early in the afternoon. Cain carried Shayna's bag, and the polyester garment bag, in for her. Telling her that Aunt Mill had insisted to leave the dress with Shayna. That it belonged to her.

Shayna was glad no one had been home when they arrived. "Will you stay?" she asked him.

They found a note that Sarah had left on the fridge for Shayna. It told her to stay home, they were going out to dinner, and that Cain could come too. If he wished.

Cain smiled at the invite, "I can't. I need to get down to the book store, and I need to get to the horses, too," he said, twisting a strand of Shayna's hair. "I don't think it would be a good idea anyway."

"Shayna agreed with him, "You're right," she said, "When will I see you?"

"I will come and pick you up, first thing in the morning." He pulled her close to him, and kissed her on the cheek. So close to her lips, that he felt a small tingling sensation. "We can do whatever you want," he said, and laughed a little. "Anything that can be done in one day, anyway."

Shayna liked the thought of this. She smiled mischeiviously, "Anything?" she asked.

"Yes." He smiled again. "I have to go."

"Okay," Shayna said, sighing. She had had an amazing time with Cain, and she didn't want it to end. Even if they were only parting for a short time.

He took her hand in his, " I will love you until the end of time," he said.

Cain turned and walked out the door. Shayna remained silent, staring after him, in the middle of the livingroom. He was angry with himself for not telling her everything he had needed to. For not telling her the one thing that would ultimately seal his fate with her. He vowed to himself, walking through her yard, to tell her on Friday or not let her change him. He wouldn't let his deceit, blur her judgement of him.

Shayna closed the door behind Cain. Her mind was focused on what to plan for them to do the next day. Oh the possibilities. She thought. She couldn't wait for the upcoming "Big Day". She didn't care about any pain, or anguish, that she would potentially go through. She would endure anything for him.

Cain's eyes immediately met Aunt Mill's, when he walked into the bookstore. She stood at the cash register shaking her head at him.

"What?" he asked.

"You didn't tell her," the woman accused, "You have to tell her everything Cain."

"I know." Cain said, "I am so ashamed of what I did." He sat down in the red velvet covered victorian chair that was next to the register. I'll tell her in the morning. I won't wait any longer." He hated living with his regretful secret everyday that he spent with Shayna.

~ 156 ~

"I hope you don't lose her Cain," Aunt Mill told him. Her eyes filled with sympathy for the, love sticken, Changeling that stood before her. "Hopefully, she has the heart to forgive you."

Chapter 13

After being forced at dinner to give up every detail of her evening, Shayna was able to get Sarah and Melina, mostly Melina, to leave her alone when the other patrons at the movie Sarah had taken them to, began shushing them. They got home late from Traverse City, and the girls told their mom "Thank you", and they all three went their separate ways in the big old house. Sarah and Shayna went to their bedrooms and Melina found the remote control, and her favorite spot on the couch, and started flipping through channels.

It was a little after midnight, and Shayna had just begun to drift off to sleep, when she heard a soft rapping noise at her window. She sat straight up in her bed, and looked towards the noise. Cain. She thought. And got up and slowly walked to the window.

Her room was dark, but when she got closer to the window, the dim light from the street, outlined a small silhouette, and she could see two small shiny black eyes looking at her. The rapping came again. She quietly opened her window and wondered, with a smile, how long she should make him wait before inviting him in. She heard him scratch at the windowsill, and knew he was getting impatient.

"You can come in," she finally said.

It was Aiden's human form, not the hawk, that entered her room.

"What are you doing here?" she whispered to him. "My mom and sister are here, and my sister is probably still awake."

"Then we better be quite. Did you have a good time last night?" he asked her, smiling.

"Of course!" she told him. "The best time of my life. Why?"

"Shayna, you can't do this!" Aiden's face suddenly turned serious. "You can't just give him your blood like this."

"How do *you* know? Can *you* read my mind?" she asked, confused.

"Oh how I wish I could. The wall in your mind is as hard to break through, as you are," Aiden said. He took her hand and led her to her bed, and had her sit down. "I was there Shayna. I followed you. I can't let you do this. I will stop him."

"Aiden, I don't think this is your decision." Shayna looked at him in the darkness, "My father would want me to be happy. I think he would approve," she said.

Aiden jumped up off the bed in a tiff, "The hell he would!" he exclaimed.

"Shh. You're going to wake them up," Shayna whispered.

Aiden knelt down on the floor in front of her, "Shayna, I didn't want to be the one to tell you this. I had hoped Cain would, but your giving me no choice," Aiden said, "I knew your father for a long time. You could say he was like a father to *me*."

"He created you?" Shayna asked.

"Yes," he answered, "He snuck up on me, one night when I was on my way home from seeing my love, Roslyn," Aiden paused, there was anger in his eyes.

~ 159 ~

"He would have killed me, but I begged him to turn me, to make me like him."

Shayna's full attention was on Aiden, he continued, "I told him about Roslyn, and what she was. I begged and pleaded for him to turn me so I could be with her forever, and he did," Aiden said, and wiped a tear from his eye. Shayna didn't even know that vampires *could* cry. "When I recovered, and I was fully immortal, I rushed to be with her. I tried to hurry, to be with her for her own change. I didn't want her to go through it without me and alone. But, when I got there," Aiden stuck his finger into the coin pocket of his jeans and pulled out a, very old looking, gold chain with a large beautiful emerald on it. "I found this next to her body on the bed."

Aiden held the necklace out to Shayna, and she took it in her hand examining it in the dark. It was ice cold it reminded her of Cain. Even in the darkness, she could tell it was a beautiful piece of jewelry.

"When I found this," Aiden began again. "I knew who had killed her. Our mother had given us these necklaces when we had reached twelve years of age. Except mine is a sapphire," Aiden had never shown another soul Cain's necklace. It had never touched any hands other than his, Cain's, and their mother's. "Up until that night, I had thought my brother to be dead. Year's of mourning him, and he came back like that." He let a tear roll down his face and drip onto his pants.

Shayna felt bad for Aiden, but it had happened so long ago, and she knew Cain didn't mean to kill Roslyn.

"When I found that necklace and picked it up, and touched the stone," Aiden said, watching Shayna hold her beloved Cain's necklace. She touched the stone, and he spoke again. "I touched it, and my mind filled with all sorts of visions. Visions of your fathers face. Visions of Roslyn helping Cain when he appeared ill. Visions of him draining every bit of life out of her, and visions of places that he must have traveled after his change. Places I never knew he had been before anyway. I think his memories were being implanted in the emerald."

"I don't see anything," Shayna said, still holding the necklace.

"They faded away many years ago," Aiden said, sounding a little disappointed, and standing up. He sat on the bed next to Shayna. He wasn't done, "I immediately went back to your father and told him what had happened to Roslyn and told him to finish what he had began in the first place." Aiden gave a little chuckle, "He refused, of course. He told me then, about Changelings, and that's how I found out what Cain is. I hate my brother. He killed the only girl I have ever loved." Aiden tightened his hands into fists, hidden next to his legs on the bed. It pained him to talk of what happened.

Before Aiden could go any further, Shayna interjected, "They had made a deal, and he got carried away." Shayna was getting annoyed with always having to defend Cain to his own brother.

"I don't care Shayna," Aiden said abruptly, "That's not my point anyway. I vowed at that time to never let him touch another Halfling Princess again. I've only failed one time," Aiden said, refering to the poor girl in the slums. "I followed him to many places.

Aiden stood up and walked to the window, and Shayna wondered if he was ever going to get to his point.

"Aiden," Shayna said quietly.

Aiden ignored her, and started talking again, "I stayed in contact with you father through out the years.

He had taught me how to be a vampire, frankly speaking. He took me under his wing," he said, "I had followed Cain to a small place in Northern California. Eureka. I think it was called." Shayna watched Aiden pace silenlty in front of the window, she let him go on, thankful he was being quiet. "I followed Cain for a couple nights, in this place, before I realized that *he* was following someone too." Aiden stopped pacing, and stared out the window.

Shayna wondered if he was going to continue. Aiden stood in front of the window, speechless, with his back to her. Then it hit her. She realized what Aiden was getting at. How Cain had known about her. Who Cain was following. What Aiden was trying to convey to her, was becoming clear.

"He was following my dad," she said. It wasn't a question, it was a realization.

Aiden turned and looked at her, giving her a nod.

"You're lying," Shayna accused him.

"I didn't say it," Aiden said.

"You're going to. But don't." Shayna stood up walked to the window too, and opened it, "Not only do I not want to hear it, I don't believe you," she gestured to the window, "Please leave."

"What am I trying to say Shayna?" Aiden asked.

"Stop!" she demanded.

"That Cain ki--," Shayna slapped Aiden across the face before he could finish. She knew she hadn't phased him, he didn't even move a muscle, but she just wanted him to stop. She didn't want to hear it, even if it *was* true."

"Just leave," she said to him.

"Fine," he whispered.

He wasn't going to stand there and torture her anymore. He moved towards the window and looked at her, while putting one leg out.

"I'm sorry, I had to be the one to tell you Shayna."

Shayna turned away from him. She was glad he was leaving.

Aiden left knowing what he had told Shayna would soon sink in. He would come back for her at a different time.

Shayna closed the window, when Aiden was out, and went back to her bed. She had a feeling that Cain was still holding something back from her. She never dreamed it could be something this horrible, and she knew deep in her heart that Aiden was telling the truth. She buried her face into her pillow and cried, her world had suddenly crashed down around her. Then the pain came. Her heart hurt, starting as a burning, then turning into a deep throbbing ache. Her heart was breaking. She couldn't believe he had done it. Even in the short period of time that Shayna had known Cain, she had truly loved him, and he lied to her and betrayed her the whole time. She sobbed hard into her pillow.

The hawk landed on an small island, that was in the middle of a lake near Shayna's house. He was pleased with himself, for accomplishing one of his goals. Get Cain out of the picture. Her father would definatly *not* approve! He thought, laughing to himself. The hawk took human form, and Aiden, walked along the beach, anticipating the events that were about to unfold. He smiled smugly to himself. He would *not* allow Cain to have Shayna's blood.

Chapter 14

Cain could see the look on Shayna's face, when he parked his BMW at the curb, and knew something was horribly wrong. He got out, and walked cautiously to the porch, where she was sitting on the swing, wondering if she already knew.

"Damn you Aiden," he muttered, under his breath, and walked up the stoop towards Shayna. He should have been the one to tell her. He should not have let it been Aiden.

Shayna stared out towards the yard and didn't even so much as blink, when Cain sat down beside her.

"Shayna, I need to talk to you," he said, hoping one last time that she didn't already know.

Shayna turned and glared at him, with eyes like daggers. He had hoped she would never look at him with such anger, and hurt. It killed him inside to see the hurt in her eyes. She did know.

"I don't want to hear anything you have to say Cain," she said coldly, "Did you think I would never find out? How could you look me in the eyes every day and let me fall in love with you, knowing, that you took the one person that I needed the most in life?" Tears began falling from Shayna's eyes.

Cain wanted to hold her, and soothe her. He didn't want to be the one hurting her.

"How was I supposed to know?" he said quietly. "He was the one that attacked me that night. He was the one person I hated in this world most, besides myself." Cain tried to take Shayna's hand, but she pulled it away and used it to wipe the tears from her face. Cain continued talking, not sure if Shayna would listen. "I didn't want to come here, but Aunt Mill told me I had to. She kept telling me not to worry about anything, and to come here," Cain said, then paused briefly. "I understand now, you are the one she has been talking about since I met her."

Shayna looked at Cain furiously with tear filled eyes. "The one, what? The one who would change you?" she asked, furious.

"No," Cain said, he didn't want her blood anymore, "I am so sorry this is happening," he shook his head, "I should have never came here."

Shayna didn't respond. She slowly stood up and walked into the house, leaving Cain sitting on the porch swing alone. She wanted him to leave. She never wanted to see him again, and she agreed, that he should have never came. She went upstairs to her room, threw herself on the bed, and buried her face into the pillow and cried.

When Shayna didn't come down for dinner, Sarah went to her room to check on her. The room was dark. Sarah turned on the lamp and could see Shayna fast asleep, on top of the covers, on the bed. Her face was swollen in a way, that Sarah knew, tears could have only done. Sarah ached for her daughter's pain, whatever it was. She kissed her lightly on her forehead, and covered her with the blanket that was at the foot of the bed.

She turned the lamp back off, and left the room. She wished she knew what had made Shayna cry hard enough to make her face swell in that way. She did know however, that Shayna would probably never tell her what it is, and that it probably had to do with Cain.

"Why are you so stubborn?" she said, out loud, and shook her head as she walked down the hall to the staris.

Shayna always liked when her dreams were at the waterfall. It usually meant her father would be there. She wondered if he ever visited Melina's dreams.

"Sometimes." She heard a familiar voice say from behind her, in response to her thought.

Shayna whirled around to face him, and to throw her arms around him. "Daddy!" she cried.

Marcus Verona held his daughter while she cried into his chest, "Everything will be okay Shayna," he told her, stroking her hair. "But you have to listen to me, he took her face in his hands and looked at her, "Go to him Shayna, he is the one for you. You have to forgive him for what he did. You must believe me."

"No," Shayna said, "He killed you," she was crying uncontrollably.

Her father wiped the tears from her face, "I killed him Shayna. I left him for dead and took his natural life. You shouldn't blame him, I don't." He pulled her close to him, her head resting on his chest again, and continued stroking her hair. "But I gave him you, and he loves you. His love for you, is as pure as love gets. You two can do great things together." He squeezed her tiny body tightly, "Go to him Shayna. He needs you. Go."

Standing atop of a huge sand dune looking out over Lake Michigan, Cain wondered if he jumped, to the rocky shore below, if he would actually die. He had no purpose, no reason to go on without Shayna.

"I should have never came here," he said, kicking at the sand.

He hated that he was making her hurt so much. A branch snapped behind him. Someone had snuck up on him. But how? He wondered. He turned around to face the intruder. A dark figure with blood red eyes stood in the darkness, red eyes fixed on Cain.

"Who are you?" Cain asked. "What do you want?"

The creature stared at Cain, with striking eyes, growling under his breath.

"Answer me dammit!" Cain yelled at it.

"I want you!" The creature of the night snarled. A deep rumble came from the hooded figures chest and it moved it's human like arm, to the side, exposing an ancient looking dagger.

Cain's eyes widened. He had only seen a dagger like it one time in his existance, and it had been in a book. The dagger was designed to kill Changelings, and he knew it. The design had been created and discovered by the father of a Halfling Princess, hundreds of years earlier. No one was quite sure what made the dagger work so effectivly, but, the pure platinum daggers, if blessed by a Roman priest, killed Changelings without fail everytime.

"You're time on this Earth is over Cain De Luca," the dark creature growled.

Cain stood motionless and the creature stalked forward, pulling the dagger out of it's sheath. The moon reflected off the shiny platinum blade, and Cain stared at it in amazmment. It was a beautiful ornate piece of weaponry, encrusted with rubies, and other gemstones.

"Are you going to run?" the snarly voice asked Cain. The creature held up the dagger and came closer.

"No," Cain answered. "I'm not. This is what I want. My time here *is* over."

The creature stood, before Cain and raised the dagger. Cain stood proud, waiting for his death. He didn't want to hurt Shayna anymore. With a quick movement and a flash of the blade, the creature plunged the dagger into Cain's chest, piercing his unbeating heart. The hooded face was only inches away from Cain's, and Cain was able to look into his blood red eyes. He could feel the poison of the cold blade entering his blood. He could see the creatures face clearly.

"You!" He sputtered as a fire erupted in his chest.

"Ahh," the creature hissed, "For all is not what it appears."

In an instant, the devil like creature thrust Cain's body over the bluff and watched him fall and hit the rocks below, with a hard thud. The dagger remained in Cain's chest, right where the creature wanted it. It hissed in delight.

"Good riddance Cain De Luca," the creature snarled, and turned, leaving the bluff.

The last thing Cain felt, was the waters of Lake Michigan seaping into his wound. It was a cold numbing feeling, that he somewhat enjoyed. He could hear the water splashing on the rocks around him, and then everything turned red, and he couldn't see or hear anything.

The red faded to black, and the Changling was gone. His existance was over. Only an empty body remained, lying on the jagged rocks, at the bottom of the dunes bluff.

Chapter 15

Shayna woke up thinking about what her father had said, but, she wasn't sure that she was quite ready to forgive Cain for what he had done. She hated feeling alone, with no one to talk to about it. Maybe she could talk to Aiden. Tell him what her father said. He probabaly wouldn't care. She thought. He hated Cain for his own reasons.

Shayna didn't hate Cain, she still loved him very much. And, she realized she did forgive him. She knew her dad was right. He was the one for her., but she wasn't ready to look him in the eyes yet. He had killed her father, she would need more time.

She opened the closet door to get some clothes and immediately saw the garment bag, which held Aunt Mill's dress. Her eyes began to tear up. She would always remember the evening on the island with Cain, no matter what happened.

She grabbed a pair of jeans, and a light pink hooded pullover cardigan, and closed the closet door. She was not looking forward to going to school, she wanted to crawl into her bed in a fetal position, and stay there forever. But as Sarah had assumed, she had been neglecting her responsibilities. She had to go.

When Cain never showed up for school, Shayna wasn't surprised. In Advaced Art, she sat in her seat alone, staring at the portrait he had drawn of her.

The final bell of the day rang, and Shayna left her class, and went to her locker to get the books she needed to complete the History assignment that she still had not turned in. She was able to get a two day extension, telling the teacher that everything was on her laptop, and her laptop wasn't working. He gave her the extension, and told her to bring the laptop in for repairs. The Art Academy had issued the laptops to the students, and handled all maintenance.

Shayna closed her locker, and to her surprise, Melina was standing on the other side of the door.

"You okay today?" she asked Shayna.

"I'm fine."

Melina knew she was lying, "Come on Shay," she put her arm around Shayna's shoulder and turned her toward the exits, "Let me give you a ride home," she said.

Shayna didn't protest, She walked with her sister out of the school, to the parking lot, holding back her tears.

As soon as the Honda was out of the parking lot, Melina started in on her.

"Shayna, what's going on? I have never seen you so happy, and now you're staying in bed all day, and your face is obviously, tear stained and swollen," Melina paused, "Did he do something to you?" she asked.

Shayna burst into tears, at the thought of Cain hurting her. What Irony. "You wouldn't understand Melina," she sobbed.

"Try me."

"I have to get over his past, and it is a very difficult thing to do," Shayna wiped more tears from her face. She was feeling vulnerable, and miserable.

"That seems pretty understandable Shay," Melina said looking at her twin awkwardly, "His past is his past, Shayna, and if you can't get over his past, you're not going to have much of a future.

Shayna looked at Melina through tears, and said, "Don't you think I've thought about that Mel? If I can't get over this, we can't have a future. And what he did is," Shayna tried to swallow a lump that had formed in her throat. She wished she could tell her twin sister what he had really done. But there was no point in making her hate him, and be in pain herself, all over again. "What he did is pretty bad," she said after a moment.

Melina knew Shayna telling her was a longshot, but she asked the obvious question, that was burning on her mind, "What did he do?" she said.

They were almost to their street. Shayna had forgotten, how quick it was, to get home in the car.

"He has killed," she said so quietly, it was almost a whisper.

But Melina heard her, and remained silent. She didn't know what to say. She knew there were circumstances when someone had to take the life of another, but she didn't know Cain's circumstances, maybe he had needed to do it. She couldn't believe Shayna had divulged this.

Shooting her a look, that Melina had never seen before, Shayna said, "Don't you ever tell anyone." The tone in Shayna's voice was threatening, and very unlike her, Melina knew she was serious, "I don't want anyone, but myself to think negatively of him."

Melina couldn't believe that Shayna was telling her as much as she had. But quite honestly, something in Melina's brain sparked with excitement when she thought of Cain as a killer. He was so handsome, and mysterious. He didn't look like a killer. The thought made him more attractive.

"I promise I won't tell," Melina said to her. Although she would tell Noah at the first chance she got, but only Noah.

They got home, and Shayna went staight up to her room to get started on her assignment. She worked for an hour, and got nothing done. Cain's face was on her mind, and she was unable to focus. She realized she didn't need time. She was ready, and she was only torturing herself, and him, by staying away. She was eternally his. She knew what she had to do. She got up from her desk, and grabbed her car keys off of the dresser, where they had been collecting dust. Without saying a word to Melina who was sitting downstairs on the couch, in her usual spot, Shayna left the house. She got in the Honda Prelude and began driving towards Cain's house. She had to go to him. She couldn't make him wait any longer.

Shayna was relieved to see Cain's car in the driveway. When he never showed up to school, she assumed he had left. But, when Aunt Mill answered the door, Shayna immediately noticed the distressed look on her face. Shayna's heart sank to her knees.

"What is it?" Shayna demanded grabbing the old woman's hands.

"Come in dear," Aunt Mill said, bringing Shayna into the foyer, and motioning for her to go to the livingroom. "Please, have a seat."

Shayna sat down on a red velvet victorian couch, the matching chair she realized, was at the bookstore.

"Where is Cain?" she asked Aunt Mill nervously. Her instincts told her that this wouldn't be good news.

The old woman sat down next to her, "I don't know," she said, and stared out the window at the barn. "He left yesterday morning, before I went to the bookstore to do inventory, and I haven't seen him since.

When I try to reach out to him, I get nothing but blackness." She looked at Shayna with frightened eyes, "Like he isn't there. I can't find him."

"What does that mean?" Shayna asked. She had an inclining, that Aunt Mill could sense and see things. She figured it out, the day Cain had said she sent him a message to go to the cemetary. Shayna could feel the tears stinging her eyes. She new something wasn't right.

"I don't know, it could mean more than one thing." Aunt Mill looked out at the barn again.

Shayna fought back tears and asked, "Like what?"

Aunt Mill took a deep breath, "It could mean he's too far away from me, it could mean he's blocked me out." She fidgited with a loose thread on the long floral dress that she wore. "Or, it could mean that he is gone," she said quietly, and looked down at her lap.

"Gone?"

Aunt Mill didn't say anything, she continued to stare at her lap.

"What do you mean gone?" Shayna asked, she needed to hear her say it. "Aunt Mill?"

The woman sighed loudly. She didn't want to see Shayna in pain, but she knew she need to tell her. "He has either left, and we'll both never see him again. He's dead, or he has changed," she said, "And, it's highly unlikely that he has changed."

Once again fighting back tears, Shayna asked, "Do you think he's dead?"

The same distressed look, she had at the door, returned to Aunt Mill's face, "I don't know," she said, "I don't know anything. That's what worries me the most. All I see is blackness." The old woman bagan to tremble.

"Would he have left because of me?" Shayna asked.

"Shayna he would die for you, and if he couldn't have you, he would want to die," Aunt Mill didn't hesitate to say, "And, yes, he would leave. What is left of his spirit would probably leave too. He doesn't want you in pain."

Shayna didn't know what to say. Cain couldn't leave her. How would she ever find him to tell him that everything would be okay, and that she forgave him. She was still his.

She sprang to her feet, "I have to go," she said.

She knew Aunt Mill would not mind if she began sobbing like a baby on her couch, but she had to get out of there.

"Thank you Aunt Mill," she said, bent down, and kissed the woman on the cheek. "I will come back soon, I promise."

Shayna didn't even make it out the door, and the tears were rolling. She had almost reached the Honda, when she heard a loud thud, coming from the barn. Obsidion. Her mind was so focused on Cain, she had forgotten about Obsidion. Without thinking, she turned and headed toward the barn.

She reached his stall, and slowly opened the door. The massive black stallion immediately began rubbing his head on her, practically knocking her over. Shayna laughed through her tears, and rubbed his neck.

"Hey boy," she said to him, laying her head against his neck. "Where is he?"

Obsidion grunted, and gently pushed his way past Shayna, and out of the open stall door.

"Hey!" Shayna called after him, "What are you doing?"

He looked back at her, with big black eyes, and headed for the open barn doors. Shayna quickly followed after him. She couldn't believe he was going to run off on her, her first time alone with him.

The horse walked out of the barn, and Shayna came out behind him, and almost walked right into him. He had taken the kneeling position she had seen him do before, and was waiting for her to mount him.

Shayna looked around the property for anyone watching, wondering if she should do it. Obsidion whinnied softlyand quietly, and Shayna finally climbed on his back. He stood upright, and Shayna gathered some of his mane at his withers, and almost simultaneously, Obsidion took off at a full run. He ran around the barn, and down the driveway, heading west towards the sun.

Shayna knew she was being stupid. She had been neglecting so much lately, and here she was riding off into the sunset on a beautiful, black stallion. Obsidion ran, and didn't stop. All Shayna could do, was lean her body down by his neck, and let the wind whip against her face, and through her hair. She realized she really didn't care where this incredible creature was taking her. She felt so free.

When they came to the top of a dune bluff over looking Lake Michigan, Obsidion suddenly came to an abrupt stop, right when Shayna was sure he was going to leap off the edge with her on his back.

It was dark, but Shayna could see so much in the moonlight. The lake looked gorgeous in the dark, hundreds of feet below her. She inhaled the fresh air and held it in her lungs, enjoying the need to breath while she could. Cain's face appeared in her mind. He was so handsome. His emerald eyes looking at her, with nothing but love in them. She felt scared.

Obsidion began to hoof the ground, and prance in place.

"Easy," she said to him.

The horse stepped towards the the edge of the bluff, then stepped back again. He continued to do it until Shayna said,

"Is there something down there?"

She started to swing her leg over his back, to take a closer look, when she and the horse both heard a deep growl from behind them. Shayna jerked her head around in the direction of growl. In the darkness, were a pair of red eyes.

Shayna gasped. *Go Sid.* She projected. Shayna never looked back as Obsidion ran past the bush that concealed the red eyes. The horse didn't stop until he had returned her to Cain's house. Whatever the *thing* had been, it did follow them, but only for a short distance. Shayna knew it was gone when she stopped hearing the growls, but she told Obsidion not to stop until he had gotten to the barn.

Obsidion was panting horribly when Shayna walked him into the barn. She took him back to his stall, and got him some fresh water. She didn't leave until his breathing had returned to normal, and he had calmed down a little.

She wasn't surprised to see the hawk sitting on top of the barn, when she climbed into her car, but she wondered how long he had been there. She nodded her head at him, acknowledging him, and started the engine and left. She had wanted to talk to Aunt Mill about what she had seen, but the house was dark when Shayna came out of the barn, and she didn't want to wake her. She drove home praying for Cain to return to her, she was already, so lost, without him.

Chapter 16

It was after midnight when Shayna finally returned home. She expected Melina to be waiting up for her, but she was asleep in her bed, snoring away. Sarah was at work, and the house was quite. Shayna went to her room, and changed into her favorite pink, plaid pajama pants. She took off her cardigan, and left the white camisole, that was underneath, on.

Her stomach growled. Eat! She thought. She went back downstairs to the kitchen, and opened the fridge to find something that looked appealing to her, to eat. She found a container labled blood sausage, and her mouth began to water. She grabbed the container, and a loaf of bread out of the bread box, and put them on the counter. She turned around, and reached up to open the cupboard, and that was when she felt it.

There was an icy feeling on her neck, and then what felt like, soft, caressing, nibbles. She turned to face her intruder, and a squeak of a scream escaped her lips, before a finger covered them.

"Shh." Standing there with a sly smile, looking almost as handsome as his brother, was Aiden, "You would think, that you being destined to be vampire soon," he said, still smiling, "That your senses would be better."

Shayna's back was to the counter, and Aiden put his arms on both sides of her, with his hands on the counter. His face was next to hers, touching hers.

"Do you trust me yet?" he whispered into her ear.

Shayna felt a little intimidated. She knew Aiden was trying to get a rise out of her, and it seemed to be working. She didn't answer him. She trusted him to take care of her, but, she didn't trust that he knew what was *best* for her.

When she didn't answer, Aiden brushed his cold face against hers, and gently, he found her lips with his. He pressed his lips hard to hers and pulled her closer to him, with his hand on the back of her neck, embracing her body and kissing her even harder.

Shayna didn't return the kiss. She broke herself loose, placing her hands on his chest and pushing back, she said, "No Aiden. I can't do this." She didn't care where Cain was. "He's coming back for me," she told Aiden.

Aiden backed away from her.

"You're right," he said, "He probably is coming back for you, but, not in the way that you think he is."

Shayna narrowed his eyes at him.

"He doesn't take rejection well," he started to tell her. "And, when he wants something, he won't stop until he has it. He wants your blood. He needs your blood. So, deny it all you want." He leaned against the opposite counter, and folded his arms, "He will be back for you, and I'm not going to let you out of my sight."

Shayna rolled her eyes but, was a little flattered by his concern, "Whatever Aiden," she said, leaning on the counter next to him, "So, tell me again, why, you're doing this for me."

Aiden inched closer to her, he liked her sweet scent. "Shortly after you were born," he said to her. "Your father came to me, in Italy, and asked that if anything were to happen to him, that I make sure you were safe from Changelings and anything else seeking your blood. He also asked me to prepare you for your eternity." Shayna felt Aiden's cold arm on her's, and goosebumps covered her body. "I promised him I would, and after I took care of his ashes, I came to find you," he said, looking down at her, "That was when you started dreaming about me."

"Why didn't you bring *me* his ashes?"

"Because. If a vampires ashes are contained and they get into the wrong hands, horrible things could be done. Especially with your *fathers* ashes."

Shayna accepted the answer, and asked, "Why doesn't Cain enter my dreams like you? And, why would my father's ashes be so special?"

Aiden laughed, "Because Cain is weak!" he said. "He needs your blood, so he can have the ability to do things, that he can't do now. He needs to change." Aiden nudged Shayna's elbow with his, "So if you're done with all the questions, we need to figure out where I'm going to keep you Friday night."

"Where you're going to keep me?" Shayna became defensive, "What are you talking about Aiden?"

"I told you," he said, and walked into the diningroom, Shayna followed. "I'm not letting you out of my sight, especially not Friday." Aiden walked to the window that looked out at the backyard, brainstorming. "What about that prom, or ball thing, at your school? We could do that." He looked at Shayna hopeful. "Those things usually go until around midnight, right?" he smiled mischeivously at Shayna, "What do you say?"

Shayna laughed at him, "No."

Aiden looked disappointed, and asked, "Why?"

"How the hell would I explain you to everyone?" Shayna said, shaking her head. "To my sister? To my mother?" She paused to think. "No!" She wouldn't budge.

"Tell them that I am Cain's brother, and that Cain is out of town, and he asked me to take you. Because he knows how much you want to go." Aiden folded his arms, he wouldn't budge either.

Shayna laughed, hard, at him, "That's funny," she said and walked back into the kitchen.

"What?" he asked, following her this time, "What's so funny?"

Shayna turned around to face him, "I have never gone to any of my school's formal functions, and, everyone knows that I'm not going to. Why would I go now? With you?" she said, and pointed at him with a scrunched her nose.

"You changed your mind," he said. His plan would go much more smoothly, if she agreed to go to the prom, with him. "It's your senior year, you don't want to miss it. Remember?"

"You do spy on me, don't you?" she said, aiming an accusing glare at him. She remembered the conversation, that she and Melina had.

"It will work," he assured her, "Your sister will buy it at least."

"Shayna groaned in frustration. "Fine!" she barked. "If it makes you feel like you're fulfilling my fathers wish, then, I'll let you take me to the formal."

"I won't bother you anymore after that. I promise," he said, crossing his heart, but winking at her too.

"Yeah right!"

Shayna had a feeling Aiden took the job her father gave him, more serious than he should.

Aidens eyes suddenly widened, and Shayna and him both heard a board above them creak.

Melina.

"You have to go," Shayna said to Aiden, and pushed him toward the back door. She could hear the footsteps getting closer to the stairs. "Now!" she insisted. She opened the back door and pushed him out. "Sorry," she told him. A mass of feathers erupted into the night sky, and Shayna closed the door, wondering how he had gotten in.

She turned around and walked out of the kitchen, just in time to meet Melina at the bottom of the stairs.

"Who's here?" Melina asked suspiciously.

"No one," Shayna answered, "It must have been the TV in the kitchen. Shayna started past her up the stairs, and Melina grabbed her arm, stopping her.

"Where did you go earlier?" Melina questioned.

"I went to Cain's. I needed to talk to him." Shayna looked down at Melina's hand, on her arm. She felt violated in a strange way.

Melina let go of her arm.

"And?" she asked curiously.

Shayna smiled at her twin "And I'm going to the Winter Formal, like you said I should." Shayna started up the stairs again, then stopped and looked back at Melina. "With his brother," she added.

"What?!" Melina blurted out, "Why not Cain, and who is his brother, and where is *he*?" she demanded.

Her and Aiden, hadn't worked out the details about him. Shayna had to think of something, fast.

"Aiden is only visiting. He goes to college out of state. Cain will be out of town on Friday, so he asked Aiden to take me," she told Melina. Proud of herself for thinking up something so fast, but disappointed in herself for lying.

~ 181 ~

Growing more suspicious, Melina asked, "Can I meet him?"

"Friday," Shayna told her, "Goodnight."

She quickly turned and rushed up the stairs. Melina stood at the bottom, her mind racing and wondering, *what in the hell,* was going on.

Melina sat down in the same chair, she had sat in the previous time that she had met Noah in the library. She had sent him a text, telling him to meet her their. She arrived first and axiously waited for him.

He strutted in, and pulled up the chair next to her, "Sup kiddo?" He tilted his fedora to greet her.

Melina took in a deep breath, "Remember, I said Shayna said a boy's name in her sleep?" Melina lowered her voice so she couldn't be heard by the other students.

Noah nodded his head, and said, "I remember."

Melina felt like she was betraying her sister, but she knew something wasn't right. "She is going to the formal, with Cain's brother Aiden," she told him.

Noah's eyes grew large. "What?" he couldn't believe what he was hearing, "Aiden is the name she said in her sleep?"

"Yeah," Melina said, "It is."

They sat in silence for a moment, while Noah processed what Melina was telling him.

"Shayna's going to the formal?" he finally said. "That's weird itself. What the hell is going on?" Noah leaned back in his chair, and put his hands behind his head.

Melina chuckled flatly, "That's what I keep wondering."

"I think I need to try to talk to her again. Maybe I can get something out of her." he said to Melina, doubting that he could.

"Good luck with that," she told him, shaking her head with the same doubt.

"Somethings not right with this scenero," a look of worry crossed Noah's face. "I have a bad feeling about all of this. Where did these guys even come from?"

"California?" Melina suggested, but really wasn't quite sure.

Noah smiled at her, he had a thought, "I know what will get Shayna's attention. You go, with *me,* to the formal."

"Why are we trying to get Shayna's attention?" Melina asked dumbfounded, "How does that help?"

"It helps me," Noah started explaining, "Take *you* to the formal." He crossed his arms in front of him, and sat looking at her, with a quirky grin.

Melina thought about what Noah was suggesting. She wouldn't tell him, but the thought of going with him, *had* crossed her mind. He was good looking, but socially, he wasn't her type. What is my type? She asked herself.

"Okay," she said, "I'll go with you.

Chapter 17

Shayna barely made it through the next day at school, without Cain. She sat in their art class, staring at her portrait, in a daze. Ms. Olson stopped her after class and asked her if she was okay. Shayna smiled politely, and told her she was fine. She lied. She was not fine. She needed Cain to come back to her. She was becoming lost without him, and couldn't believe that she had let Aiden talk her into going to the Winter Formal. Am I going crazy? She wondered.

She sat on the porch swing alone. Both Melina and Sarah were at work, Cain was gone, and who knew where Aiden was. Shayna thought about what Aiden had said about Cain coming back for her blood. He could have it. She wanted Cain to have her blood. He needed it. Maybe she shouldn't be going along with Aiden's charade. She thought. What was she doing?

She thought about her birthday. She wished she knew what was going to happen to her. She had a feeling she wouldn't be going anywhere other than her room for a while, after the fateful day. Especially if Cain didn't return.

Noah's El Camino pulled up to the curb, and Shayna wasn't surprised. His face had popped into her mind on and off through out the day, and she sensed he would be coming to see her. He walked up the steps, and sat on the swing next to her. Both of them sat in silence, staring across the street. Shayna couldn't take it any longer, she knew Noah had come over for a reason.

"What is it Noah? I know you didn't come over, just to sit here with me."

Noah turned and looked at her. He could see what Cain and Aiden would want from her. She was gorgeous.

"What the hell is going on with you Shayna?" he asked, glaring at her, "And don't tell me "nothing." You know I'm not stupid."

Shayna didn't know how or where to start. If there was one person she wished she could tell her secrets to, it was Noah. But she didn't think she could. She knew deep down that if she wanted to remain friends with him, that one day, he would have to know.

She had to say it, she didn't know what else *to* say, "Nothing. Melina and I talked the other day, and she said I should go to at least one formal before we graduate. So I asked Cain to take me." Shayna wished the questions would stop, so that the lies would stop.

"But Cain's not taking you," Noah pointed out.

"No, he's out of town, and Aiden's visiting, so he asked him to take me," she said sticking to the original lie.

All Noah could do was look at her blankly. He knew he wasn't going to get much more out of her, and it drove him crazy to know she was lying to his face.

"Would you just talk to me?" he pleaded with her. He couldn't give up.

Shayna closed her eyes briefly, and took in a deep breath. The air was chilly, and smelled sweet, "You wouldn't understand Noah," she said, with a soft sigh. "But, I promise, I'm fine."

"Maybe I would understand Shay," he insisted, "Try me."

"Not now," Shayna said.

"When?" Noah was frustrated, "Why can't you just tell me what is going on, and where *is* Cain, anyway?"

"I wish it was that easy. Why is it such a big deal anyway?" Shayna was growing frustrated herself. All the interrogations from him and Melina were getting exhausting, "Just let it go Noah."

Noah stood up in a huff, "Dammit Shay! Your so stubborn!" He started off of the porch, "When you're ready for me to understand, you know where to find me."

Shayna let Noah leave, and didn't try to stop him. She wanted him to stay, and keep her company, but, not if he was only going to keep invading her buisiness. She hated distancing herself from him. He probably would understand. She thought, realizing that she *was* stubborn.

The smell of bacon filling the house woke Shayna up out of another dreamless sleep. She loved when Sarah woke up early, and surprised her and Melina with breakfast. Shayna quickly got dressed and went down stairs, but to her surprise Melina, was already gone.

"Where's Mel?" she asked Sarah, and sat down at the bar that seperated the kitchen from the diningroom.

"She left early," Sarah answered, and flipped the pancakes she was making, "I want to talk to you Shayna Marie."

Shayna rolled her eyes, leaned back in the bar stool, and crossed her arms, "Oh God, what?"

"Shayna this is serious," Sarah said, putting the pancakes on a plate. She brought them to the bar. "I know things are going to be different when you turn eighteen, but you still need to take your responsibilities serious." She grabbed the bacon and eggs from the counter and brought them to the bar also. "When was the last time you went to the waterfall to draw?"

Shayna was growing defensive, "There hasn't been any snow," she said, "I am trying to capture *all* of the seasons."

"Okay," Sarah wasn't done, "Did you get your transcripts?"

"Yes."

Sarah raised an eyebrow, and put her hands on the counter, "Did you send them off?"

Shayna looked down at her plate, and poured syrup on her pancakes.

"No," she said quietly.

"What about your History paper?" Sarah asked.

Shayna jumped off the stool, "Crap!" She hadn't finished the assignment. She grabbed the rest of the bacon off of her plate. "I have to go."

"You can take my car," Sarah said, although she was disappointed in her daughter, "The keys are by the door."

Shayna sprinted for the livingroom.

"Shayna!" Sarah called after her.

Shayna stopped and turned to look at her mom.

"This is *exactly* what I'm talking about." She had a stern look on her face, and Shayna knew she was upset with her.

"I get it mom. I'm sorry," Shayna was embarassed. She grabbed her backpack, and her mothers keys, and left.

Shayna had just finished wrapping up her History assignment in the school library, when she heard two familiar voices. Melina and Noah. She was shocked when she realized that they had come to library to discuss her, and if she could hear them, then other students might too. She stuffed her books into her backpack, stood up silently, and walked around to the other side of the bookshelf that seperated them.

Melina's eyes grew very large when they met Shayna's.

Noah whipped his head around to see what Melina was gawking at.

"Uh oh," he said. They were caught.

Shayna turned and walked away. She didn't have time to argue with them, and didn't want to.

"Shay!" Melina called.

Shayna didn't look back. Who cares? She thought. Let them talk about me. She left the library, and headed to her first class. Her assignment was complete, but she knew she would receive a lower grade, simply, because it had been late. Her heart told her that Cain still would not be at school, and her heart was right. She decided to stop at 'Between the Lines' on her way home.

Shayna loved the atmosphere in the little bookstore. It felt almost like a library in a church, or a castle. Something from midevel times. Aunt Mill was in the back of the shop when Shayna entered, but came to the front within moments of the door closing.

The old womans face lit up with joy when she saw Shayna, and she hugged her. Aunt Mill smelled of lemon and spice. An aroma Shayna loved smelling on the older woman.

"I'm so glad you stopped in," she said.

"I'm sorry about the other night," Shayna said sitting down in the victorian chair by the register, "This has a been so much to take in."

"I understand dear," Aunt Mill looked at her sympathetically. "It is a lot."

"Have you heard anything?"

Aunt Mill sighed, "I still only see darkness." there was concern in her eyes. "But something is going to happen Shayna. Something big."

Shayna staightened her back, "What do you mean?"

"I don't know. It is something that I have been sensing lately, but I can't decipher, whether it's good or bad." She turned toward the window and looked out, "Maybe both," she whispered.

Shayna didn't know what to say. The only question she could think of, she dreaded asking, "Do you think it involves me?"

Aunt Mill looked at the floor, "Yes."

Shayna took in a deep breath, "Do you see anything else? How am I involved?" Shayna was slowly starting to dislike her life, especially with Cain gone.

"Oh Shayna dear," Aunt Mill took Shayna's hand, "I really wish that I knew more. Really."

"Should I be scared?" Shayna asked her. She knew her life was about to take a major turn, but she didn't ever expect it to be for the worse. She knew how happy, her father was in life.

"Maybe," Aunt Mill shook her head in frustration. "I can't tell. It really discerns me that I can't tell. I think it's because I can't see him. She sighed again, and stared out the window.

Shayna looked at her. It seemed a foggy haze had cast over Aunt Mill's eyes.

"Aunt Mill?" Shayna said wearily.

The old woman seemed to snap back to reality.

"Surround yourself with friends Shayna, yes that's a good idea."

Shayna wasn't sure what had happened. Maybe she had a vision, she thought. She smiled at her and blinked her eyes.

"Where my dress dear, you'll be the bell of the ball."

Shayna blushed behind her smile. She was growing very fond of Aunt Mill.

"Thank you," she told her, and stood up and kissed the fragile womans cheek.

The night was coming soon. Shayna lay in bed overwhelmed with anticipation and anxiety, and a sickening feeling that Cain was never coming back. She couldn't help but think about what Aunt Mill had said, and that just made the anxiety worse. She lay there and hoped, that Aiden would make sure that everything would be fine. She finally fell asleep, reeading Utopia, and it wasn't long after that she was dreaming.

Marcus Verona squeezed his daughter's hand. They were standing on the bluff that Obsidion had brought Shayna to. The sky was blood red with the setting sun over Lake Michigan.

"The time is coming, my daughter," he said, "I wish I could have prepared you for this, before I left. I don't know what I was thinking." He turned to face her, "The truth is, I should have never left you. I should have stayed, or taken you with me." His eyes were sad.

"Dad, I'm not going to hold it against you," Shayna said to him, "You did what you thought you had to do," she gave him a tight hug. "I think I'm going to be fine." She knew she would be. She was strong, and she was going to make the best of the new life that was awaiting her.

"Shayna," Marcus knew his daughter's heart was breaking, "Look into your heart, and you will find Cain." He gently nudged her towards the edge of the bluff. Shayna was afraid of heights, but began to step forward. It's only a dream, her mind told her. There must be a reason her father brought her to this place.

There was a growl behind them.

Shayna spun around. Not again! Her father was gone, standing about ten feet or so away from her, was a dark hooded figure with red, glowing eyes.

Shayna screamed, and could feel herself actually scream in her sleep.

"What do you want?" she demanded, trembling.

The hooded figure stood staring at her, silent, and motionless.

"Wake up! Wake up! Wake up!" Shayna cried to herself.

Finally the figure moved. It stalked toward her, and started moving it's hand to it's hood.

Wake up! Shayna screamed in her head.

She opened her eyes, right as Melina burst through her door, Sarah running in immediately behind her. Shayna sat up in her bed covered in sweat, heart pounding, and gasping for breath. She had been more scared than she realized.

Sarah rushed to Shayna's side, hoping Melina, hadn't seen, what she had seen.

"Are you okay?" she asked Shayna, smoothing back her hair, she glanced at Melina briefly.

Shayna's eyes were fixed on Melina's frightened face. "I'm fine," she said, trying to stablize her breathing. Melina was standing in the doorway, staring at her, like she had seen a ghost.

"You sure?" Sarah asked.

"Yes," Shayna looked from her mother, to her sister, then back to Sarah again. "It was only a dream," she told them, trying to reassure them, that she *was* fine.

"Okay," Sarah said, and stood up. "Goodnight," she walked to the door, and put her hand on Melina's arm. "C'mon."

Melina stood, staring at Shayna still, with the same frightened expression. Sarah pulled her out of the door way, and closed the door.

"Mom, what was wrong with her eyes?" Shayna heard Melina ask their mother through the door.

Shayna didn't hear the answer. They must have stepped away from the door before Sarah answered. Shayna realized she was shaking, and lay back down in her bed. Too afraid, to fall back to sleep. She lay in the dark with her eyes closed, fighting sleep, until she felt the sun on on her face through the bit of her drapes that were open. She wondered the whole time about what had been wrong with her eyes. Had they looked like Cain's eyes? She thought.

Chapter 18

The board in her closet seemed more tough than normal to pry up. Shayna was looking for any information she could find in the books she had, about the creature that had been in her dream, but she came up empty handed.

She was all grimey from her sweaty sleep, and got in the shower. Melina came in to talk to Shayna, and the first thing she noticed was the board in the closet that was pried up. Then she saw the books on Shayna's bed. Shayna was still in the shower. Melina walked to the bed and picked up one of the books.

"Halfling Princess?" she read aloud, and found the first chapter, and started to read, "What the…?"

She put the book back down on the bed, and picked up the one next to it. Opening it randomly.

"Oh my god," she said, and with a trembling hand, she put that book back on the bed.

The water in the bathroom turned off, and Melina backed out of Shayna's room. This isn't true. She thought, closing the door. It's not possible. Melina ran down the stairs and grabbed her phone out of her bag, and texted Noah to meet her at Dutch Cup, before her shift.

Shayna walked into her room, and her nostrils burned with the smell of Melina's freshly applied perfume. She glanced at her closet, and then the bed.

"Dammit," she said quietly.

She was mad at herself for not thinking to put her stuff away. She wondered what Melina had seen. She screwed up, but she knew it was only a matter of time anyway. She wasn't going to stress over it. She wasn't looking forward to another day without Cain. She only had one more day of being mortal left, of being the Shayna that everyone knew.

With a towel wrapped around her, she turned and looked at her reflection in the mirror. She wondered if she would look different. She let the towel drop to the floor and continued to examine herself. She closed her eyes, and saw Cain's face. She began to cry. She had been able to refrain herself from crying for a couple of days. It didn't suit her. But the longer Cain was gone, the weaker she felt against the burning behind her eyes. She tried to imagine him holding her, but she could only feel the pain of her heart breaking. Reluctanlty she got dressed. She replaced the board in her closet, and put the shoebox, that had been inside, in the bottom of her laundry basket with a pile of dirty clothes on top of it, in case Melina was snooping later. Shayna knew her ignorance had been foolish.

The thought of Melina and Noah's little detective game made Shayna laugh as she walked across the yard, when she left the house. Melina had apparently gotten in the habit of leaving Shayna to walk to school. Shayna wouldn't say anything though, as long as there was very little snow, she didn't mind the fresh air.

She walked toward the road and realized that it was her last day of school, before she turned. Due to the Winter formal, and Conferences, there was no school Friday. The anxiety became overpowering. She had to sit down on the curb until the feeling passed.

Noah arrived at Dutch Cup, and could see Melina sitting at a table outside waiting for him. Before he could even sit down with her, she blurted out,

"Shayna's a vampire!"

She had a horrified look on her face, but Noah thought she was joking. He laughed.

"I'm dead serious," Melina said. The expression on her face changed, "Last night she woke up screaming, and when I opened her door," Melina stopped, she looked to Noah, like she might cry, "Her eyes were silver."

"What do you mean, silver?" Noah asked confused.

"The blue of her eyes, was really bright, almost white," she tried to explain. "I opened the door, and when the light shone in, I could see her eyes, they looked silver in the darkness. It scared the crap out of me," Melina's expression began to relax a little. "This morning, I found books about vampires on her bed, and, I'm pretty sure that she hides them in the floor, in her closet."

"You are serious," Noah said, coming to the realization. "She's a vampire?"

"According to this book, not quite yet," she told him. "This book says, that my father was a vampire too."

"This is crazy," Noah's mind was racing, he sat back in his seat.

"This *is* crazy!" Melina agreed. "Do you believe me?' she asked Noah.

He looked at her, "Well, you obviously believe yourself, it's kind of hard, not to believe you. Does your mom know?"

Melina shrugged her shoulders, "I don't know," she said. "But I think she knows something. I asked her about Shayna's eyes, because I'm pretty sure she saw them too, but she told me it was probably an optical illusion, or the light," Melina rolled her eyes. "I don't buy that garbage. I know what I saw."

"Wow," Noah was trying to take in, what he was hearing, "This is what I wouldn't understand."

"What?"

"Well," Noah's said, squinting his eye, so he could see Melina through the sun. "Yesterday, when I tried to talk to her, she said I wouldn't understand. This is what she what she was talking about." Noah was a very open minded individual, and was beginning to understand a lot, "Wow." he said again, "This is kinda cool."

"Shut up Noah," Melina said, poking at him. Melina did secretly agree with him, something she found herself doing a lot. "This is serious," she couldn't believe that they were really talking about her twin sister being a vampire. "Am I dreaming?" she asked him.

"What about Aiden and Cain? Where do they fit into the picture?" Noah asked.

"I don't know, we will still have to figure that one out," Melina answered.

They sat outside the coffee shop together until Melina started her shift. Noah went home and got on his computer, he had some research to do. Melina had told him everything that she had read, which wasn't much, and he was going to investigate as much as he could. He felt as though him and Melina, were starting right back at 'square one'. But at least they had a lead to go on.

Shayna sat in the window seat in her bedroom, staring out at the night. She would be lying to herself, if she tried to pretend that she wasn't genuinally scared about what the day to come would bring. She looked into the darkness, praying that he would return to her, and knowing that Aiden was wrong. She hoped that what Aunt Mill was anticipating to happen would all be good. She wondered where Aiden was. Did he disappear too? She thought. Deep down she wished, *he* had never came to Michigan. Cain wouldn't be gone.

"You're wrong, Aiden," she said out loud, "I know it."

The Winter Formal came to her mind. She wasn't even sure if she knew how to dance. When Shayna and Melina had seen each other in gym class, Melina had insisted, that she would help get Shayna ready. Shayna reluctantly agreed. She needed the time with her twin sister, she didn't know when she would have it again.

Shayna closed the drapes and climbed into her bed, the purple satin comfoter was cool on her skin. She turned off the light, and rested her head on the pillow.

"I'm ready," she said into the darkness, and closed her eyes.

The waters of Lake Huron were a beautiful turquoise blue, and the beach was beautiful. Cain's face was as handsome as ever. Shayna lept into his arms, and kissed his face all over. She was so happy to see him, even if it was only in a dream.

They were on the beach on Mackinac Island.

"Shayna, I'm coming back for you," he said, holding her face in his hands and looking into her eyes. "You are my princess, and I haven't forgotten you. You are all that I know now."

Everything seemed so real to Shayna. His touch still felt like cold electricity. She held him. She refused to let go.

"I promise, just a little longer," he said, "And, we'll be together again," he tightened the hold he had on her petite body.

He feels so real, he smells so real. She thought.

"I love you Cain. I miss you so much," she kissed him more. She even dared to kiss him on the lips, but to her disappointment there was no uncontrolable effect in her dream. "I forgive you. I understand now," she said, and buried her face in his chest. "I don't want to be without you anymore."

He stroked her curly, chocolate hair, "Soon Princess, soon."

He gently laid her down on the sandy beach and began to kiss her, and Shayna entered into a whole different state of dream.

There was a smile on Shayna's face when she awoke. She could still smell him. She breathed in deeply. She had no idea how the day would end, but she was certain that Cain was going to return to her.

She got dressed, and met Melina downstairs. The plan was to go into Traverse City to get there hair and nails done. Shayna had protested, she had thought that Melina was going to do everything herself, at home. In the end Melina won.

"No make up," Shayna said, after she gave in. Melina agreed.

They drove down South Long Lake Road, and Shayna noticed that Melina seemed withdrawn. After much thought, and consideration, Melina couldn't take it any longer.

"Is it true Shay?" she asked her twin.

Shayna wasn't sure what she was talking about, she had a good idea, but continued to play stupid.

"Is what true?" she asked.

Melina glanced over at Shayna, trying not to take her eyes off the road.

"What I read in those books?"

Shayna was at a loss for words. She hadn't expected to be having this conversation with Melina, not so soon anyway. She was guessing that if Melina knew, that Noah knew as well. Melina seemed to be pretty calm though.

"Are you okay?" Shayna asked her twin. There was no point in trying to lie, and she was glad that it had came to this.

Melina started crying, her brain screamed; My sister is a vampire!

"Are *you*?" Melina sobbed.

"I'm scared shitless Mel!" Shayna started crying too, "I don't know what's going to happen to me after tonight. I'm not going to be *me* in the morning," she said wiping tears from her face.

"It's going to happen tonight?" Melina asked. She felt like she might go in to shock, "Tonight?" she repeated quietly.

Shayna nodded and wiped more tears. "Uh-huh."

Melina pulled the car over to the side of the road and hugged Shayna. They both cried and held each other.

"Why didn't you tell me?" Melina asked, pulling back onto the road.

Shayna flipped down the visor to use the mirror, and looked at her face, wiping the remaining tears away.

"I don't know. I guessed I wasn't sure I believed it myself," she said, "But then Cain showed up, and he knows what I am. It kind of made it hard not to believe it then."

"Is Cain a vampire too?" Melina asked. She was glad, and surprised that Shayna was finally opening up to her.

Shayna wasn't sure if she should answer truthfully, but she did, "Yes," she said quietly, "He is."

Melina stared ahead at the road, she wasn't sure if she could take anymore for the day. She sighed, and kept her eyes focused.

"I'm not leaving your side Shayna," she said, "I'll take you home after the formal, and stay with you," she paused, "If you'll let me."

The tears started to flowing again, followed by anxiety. Shayna was emotionally drained. She hoped she was going to be strong enough for the night. Melina started crying again too.

"I love you Shay," Melina was able to get out a laugh through her sobs, "And, as long as you don't try to drink my blood, I will always be here for you, and will help you anyway I can."

They pulled into the Grand Traverse Mall's parking lot, and Shayna took and squeezed Melina's hand.

"Mel, I will tell you everything I possibly can, after the formal," she said to her, "But for the rest of the day, let's just try to have a good time."

She hoped Melina would be able to pull herself together enough to enjoy the rest of the day, so they could have fun together.

"I would like that," Melina said and hugged Shayna.

They got out of the car, and walked inside toward Regis Salon.

Shayna added, 'You're going to tell Noah, aren't you?"

"Yep," Melina answered right away, "Unless you want to."

Shayna rolled her eyes, "Go ahead," she said, "You probably already told him anyway."

With a proud smile, Melina said, "Yep."

Chapter 19

The waters of Lake Michigan weren't quite freezing, but they were colder than his unbeating heart. He could feel the sun shining down on his face, and could hear the slushie water splashing around him. Cain slowly opened his eyes.

Everything was a little blurry at first, but it all slowly came into focus. He was staring up at the bluff, that he had been thrown from, the sun blinding him. He looked at his chest. The platinum dagger remained protruding there. He reached for the blade, his arm stiff as he moved it, and pulled it out with a quick jerk. He yelled out in agonizing pain, and pushed himself up into a sitting position, ripping his shirt open. The wound from the blade healed right before his eyes. He examined the dagger. It is definitely platinum, but how am I not fully dead? He wondered.

Many things could kill a Changeling a lot easier that a full blood. But a blessed platinum blade of any style should do the job immediately, and without fail.

"How is this possible?"

Cain managed to stand up. He looked around him. He was stuck where he was, surrounded by towering bluffs. The only way out was up or through the water. He would go up. Cain looked at the blade on the dagger again. Everything about it looked perfect, he didn't understand.

Suddenly an image of a face appeared in his mind. She was perfect, and looked like a Princess.

"Shayna," he whispered her name, "I have to get out of here."

Cain felt a surge, of what felt like adrenaline, rush through his body. He had to get to Shayna, and fast. He frantically looked around for another way to get to the top of the bluff. He had no other option. He stuck the dagger in his boot, and began to climb the sandy wall.

The girl staring back at Shayna looked like a goddess. Shayna couldn't believe that she was looking at herself.

Melina had the stylist, put most of Shayna's thick curly hair, into a french twist, leaving the rest of her dark curls falling around her face and onto her shoulders.

"Your not a little girl anymore," she said to her reflection.

Melina had talked Shayna into wearing a little mascara and a soft pink lip gloss. When Shayna hadn't been looking, Melina threw a handful of silver glitter on her. Shayna noticed the glitter later, but didn't mind. She liked the effect it added, and she didn't want to fight with Melina over glitter.

Sarah had gotten called into work, and Shayna was upset that she wasn't going to get to see her. She wasn't even sure if she had told her mom that she was going to the formal. She was anxious to get the evening over with. She didn't know when Aiden was going to pick her up, or what he would be driving. She hadn't seen him since the night that they had made their plans, and she was starting to wonder if he was still coming.

When Noah had picked Melina up, his jaw about hit the ground, when he saw Shayna. Shayna was glad to see Noah and Melina together. She would have never, in a million years, have thought of the two of them together, but once she saw it she thought they kind of fit.

Melina had not wanted to leave Shayna behind, but Shayna insisted that they go, since they had dinner plans. She promised to catch up with them at the formal.

She stood examining herself in the mirrow. She was proud of the young woman she had turned into. She looked amazing. She wanted to stop in so that Aunt Mill could see her, but she was pretty sure taking Aiden over, would not be acceptable. She smiled at the girl looking back at her in the mirror. Her eyes sparkled. More blue than ever.

A horn honked outside, and Shayna made her way to the window, and looked down at the street. Aiden was climbing out of a little silver sportscar, wearing an all black tuxedo. He was headed toward the front porch.

Shayna looked at herself one last time, and said, "Here I go," to herself.

She started downstairs to the door, taking a deep breath. She stepped off of the bottom stair, and pulled the heavy cherrywood door open. Aiden stood there grinning, with a bouquet of beautiful red roses in one hand, and a purple and silver corsage, in the other. His eyes lit up when he saw Shayna. The smile on his lips grew larger.

"I'm speechless," he said, "You look magnificent." He breathed her in, and licked his lips, "Are you ready?" he asked her.

Shayna returned the smile. "Thank you," she said softly, "Yes."

"Shall we then?" Aiden said, and extended his arm out to her.

Shayna stepped onto the porch, and shut the door behind her. Aiden took her wrist and put the corsage on it. They walked down the stoop together, and Aiden put his arm around her, handing her the bouquet.

"They don't compare to your beauty, but they smell as wonderful as you do," he told her.

"Thank you Aiden."

"Smell them," he insisted, moving her hand that was holding the roses, to her face.

Shayna leaned her face down towards the bouquet, and smelled the flowers. They did smell wonderful.

"You didn't have to do all of this Aiden." Shayna said, and then stumbled a little.

Aiden caught her, and held her up by her arm, and said, "Yes I did."

Shayna stumbled again, but Aiden had a firm grasp on her, and continued to hold her up. Everything began to spin around her. Faster and faster. Just breathe. She told herself. The only thing she was able to focus on, was Aiden's smiling face *and* his red eyes.

He opened the passenger door, "Don't be scared," he told her.

Shayna was paralyzed, she couldn't even open her mouth. Aiden was the only thing keeping her standing. He sat her down in the car, and gently leaned her back onto the seat. He was still smiling. A metallic taste began forming in Shayna's mouth, and her ears began to ring. Every part of her body was numb, and her eyes became heavy. Aiden shut the door, and walked around the car to the drivers side. Her were eyes comlpetely closed when he climbed in, and there was a single tear falling down her cheek.

The bluff had proven to be more difficult of an obsticle, than Cain had anticipated. He was only able to get about halfway up, before he lost his grip, and fell back to the rocky shore below. He repeated his attempt, but he kept falling and hitting the ground, landing on his feet. This gave him an idea. He started back up the wall of the bluff, and when he got as far as he knew he could go, he let go. When he was about to hit the ground, he bent his knees, and when he felt the earth beneath him, he immediately sprang up. He was in the air, soaring up along side the bluff. He used his legs to help him run up the side of the wall. His plan worked. About twenty feet from the top of the bluff, he was able to grab on to the roots of the growth below the sand, that were dangling down, and pull himself up.

Shayna's face in his mind, he made it to the top, and pulled himself over the ledge. He stood on his feet, and he heard Aunt Mill's voice in his head immediatly.

"The Winter formal. Hurry."

Everything came back to Cain all at once, in a whirlwind of memories and emotion. He had to get to Shayna. She was in more danger, than Cain had been to her. He started to run east, he couldn't waste any time.

Cain burst through the doors of the grand hall at the art academy. He had to find Shayna before it was too late. It took him no time at all to get to the Center For The Arts, once the panther took over. He scanned the great room for Shayna, but could not see her. He tried to find her scent, amongst her dancing classmates, but he found nothing. They're not here. He thought to himself. He was eager to find her, and frustrated that he had let this happen.

Suddenly Melina was in his line of vision and was walking right towards him, with Noah by her side. Cain was amused that Melina's thoughts of him were so scrambled, and he was relieved that she already knew about Shayna.

"Where is my sister?" Melina asked him leaning close to him, so he could hear her over the music. She didn't realize it was unecessary. The look on Cain's face, made Melina instanly worry. "What?" she asked him.

"I don't know." He looked at both Melina and Noah, "But we need to find her."

"Wait, what?" Noah interrupted. He couldn't hear them.

Melina began to shake, "What is going on Cain? Where is my sister?"

Cain looked at Noah, and leaned close to him, so Noah could hear him, "Do you have a car?"

Noah nodded.

"Cain?" Melina said, "Answer me."

"We have to go now, we have to get to my place. I'll explain in the car."

Cain turned and walked toward the exit, he wasn't about to wait for Melina and Noah. Although it would be helpful, he didn't need Noah's car. He would find Shayna on his own, if he had to.

Cain walked out of the school building, into the parking lot, followed by Noah and Melina. He hadn't been surprised when they had joined him in the hallway.

They arrived to Cain's house, and Cain effortlessy carried Melina into the house. Noah and Aunt Mill moved the coffee table out of the way, so that Cain could lay her down on the couch.

"Oh dear," Aunt Mill said. "Poor thing," she felt Melina's head, "She'll be fine, I'll go whip something together, that will wake her right up." The sweet woman smiled politely at Cain and Noah, and excused herself to the kitchen.

Melina had fainted in the car. Cain had been explaining everything to her and Noah, and apparently, him killing her father, and Shayna agreeing to exchange blood with him, had been too much for Melina to handle, and she lost consciousness.

Noah hadn't taken his eyes off the road, or said a word, while they drove to Cain's house. He just drove and absorbed everything that Cain was telling them.

With Aunt Mill out of the room, Noah looked at Cain, and asked, "So, what does all of this mean? What does Aiden want with Shayna?"

Cain shook his head, and looked at the ground. He was ashamed that he had allowed Aiden to fool him the way he had.

"I don't even know how I am alive right now," Cain told Noah, "I'm pretty sure that I changed, but I don't know how," he gestured to the empty chairs in the livingroom. "You can sit down.

Noah wasn't sure what to do. Although he felt oddly comfortable around Cain, the only other vampire he had known, was Shayna and Melina's father. But he hadn't known then,that he was a vampire. He was a nice man. Noah thought about Marcus Verona. Maybe I don't have to be scared. He assumed to himself.

"Never underestimate a vampire," Cain told him immediately, looking staight into his eyes and catching him off guard, "You should always be afraid."

"Holy crap!" Noahs mouth gaped wide open, "You just read my mind. How the hell?"

Cain nodded, and Aunt Mill returned with a small silver cup, that was steaming from the top.

"Cain dear," she said, "Sit her up."

Cain rushed to Melina and sat her up, like Aunt Mill had instructed. The fragile looking woman put the cup under Melina's nose, so that the steam filled her nostrils. Almost instantaneously, Melina's eyes popped wide open. She looked around at the faces surrounding her. When she saw Noah, the tears started to flow.

"This is a nightmare," she cried, "It can't be real," she put her face in her hands, and sobbed harder.

Noah sat down next to her and put his arm around her to console her, and Aunt Mill looked Cain up and down suspiciously.

"Well, look at you," she was smiling from ear to ear, "No wonder I couldn't find you. I wasn't looking for *you*."

"How did it happen?" Cain said, desperate for a logical answer.

Aunt Mill went to an old victorian style desk that was in the foyer, and brought back a book, and handed it to Cain. The book was old, and bound in ancient leather. Cain tried, but he couldn't make out the Italian name that was on the cover.

Sitting with Melina on the couch, Noah watched their every move.

"An old friend out in California, was able to track it down. He had it overnighted to me. It arrived just today," Aunt Mill knew Cain didn't have time to read it, but she had already gotten through most of it herself, "You fell in love with her Cain. You would do anything in the world for her, except take her blood. But the most important part is, that she loved you in return," Aunt Mill turned and looked at Melina, and Melina lifted her head off of Noahs shoulder returning the gaze, "That's how you changed," Aunt Mill said turning back to Cain.

"You really do love her? Don't you?" Melina said.

Cain nodded his head to Melina. "I do, yes," he said, but quickly turned his attention back to Aunt Mill, "Where is she? Can you find her?"

Aunt Mill closed her eyes. At least a minute passed, until she began to speak, "I see water, and I see white," Aunt Mill said. "White velvet. I can feel it in my hand."

Cain was confused, and getting impatient, time was running out.

"I know where she is," Melina said, unexpectedly. Everyone turned and looked at her, "She's on the island, Mackinac Island," Melina tried to stand up, but felt dizzy, and quiclkly sat back down. "She told mom and I all about it. Everything in her room was white and the bed was white velvet," Melina looked at Cain, "It's surrounded by water. She's on the island, in that room."

Cain turned for the door, and Noah stood up.

"I'm going with you," he told Cain.

Cain stopped and turned around, "No," he said to Noah as firm as he could.

"Melina, you stay here with…with…uh," Noah looked at the old woman.

"You can call me Aunt Mill."

Noah gave Aunt Mill an embarassed smile, and looked back to Melina.

"With Aunt Mill," he looked back to Cain, who was opening the front door, "I'm going with you."

"No, we don't have enough time," Cain said, turning around to face Noah. "It's almost nine already, and it will take close to three hours to get there driving."

"Not the way Noah drives," Melina interjected.

Noah looked at Cain and smiled. Melina was right.

"Let's go," Cain said to Noah. He knew Melina wasn't lying about the kid's driving, and he didn't have time to stay and argue.

They walked out the door, and Noah felt safe leaving Melina with Aunt Mill. Cain sent Noah to the car and then rushed to the barn, he desperatly needed to feed, before they left.

Cain and Noah arrived in Mackinaw City right before eleven o'clock. Noah found a ferry line, Shephler's Ferry, and turned into the parking lot.

"How are we going to get out there?" Noah asked, looking out at the lights of the Grand Hotel, "None of the ferry's are running, this late."

Cain climbed out of the car.

"We're not taking a ferry," he said.

Cain walked to the marina and began examining the different boats, Noah followed closely behind.

"Well?' Noah huffed, "What *are* we taking?"

"That," Cain said, pointing at a large boat named Gilly-ga-loo.

Noah looked at the boat suspiciously. It was about forty feet long, about the length of one of the ferry's, but not as big,

"Is it yours?"

Cain walked out onto the dock, "No," he said.

"Who's is it?" Noah said, running, catching up to him on the dock.

"I don't know," Cain shrugged his shoulders, and jumped onto the deck of the boat. "Can you make it?" he asked Noah.

"I think I got it," Noah said, and jumped onto the boat alongside Cain.

Noah walked to the bow, and Cain went to the helm. Noah wasn't surprised, when Cain had the motor running within seconds. The boat was fast, taking only about ten minutes to bring them to the west side of the island, where the Grand Hotel was. Cain was able to bring the boat close enough to the island, that when they jumped into the freezing waters of Lake Huron, the were only waist deep.

They walked out of the water, onto the beach that Cain and Shayna had just been walking on the week before.

"There is a door on the east side of the hotel that leads to the kitchen," he told Noah, "If it's not open, it is unlocked. If she is in that room, the room number is 334." they walked toward the hotel together, "Go," Cain instructed, "If you get to the stables, you've gone too far."

"What are you going to do?" Noah wasn't sure what he would do if he got to Shayna first.

"Don't worry about me. Just go," Cain said, and he started to sprint toward the back of the hotel, and out of Noah's sight.

Noah wasn't sure exactly what he had gotten himself into. He was on a mission for a vampire, to save a vampire, from a vampire. Maybe it is all a dream. He thought.

Chapter 20

The dull red glow, surrounded by bright white was blinding to Shayna. Her eyes fluttered open, and slowly began to adjust to the light. She looked around, barely able to move her head. Unbelievably, she was back on the island. This time instead of roses, there were white candles, burning throughout the room. She realized that the flames from the candle, were the red glow. Everything had gone horribly wrong. Her head was pounding, and she hopelessly wondered where Aiden was. He was supposed to protect her from Cain, to stop this from happening, and make sure it didn't happen at all.

A dark hooded figure stepped into the room from the balcony, and walked toward the bed.

"You're awake," he said, and sat on the bed beside her.

He put his hand on her thigh, and Shayna trembled with fear. The only thing going through her mind, was that, Aiden was supposed to protect her from this. She had trusted that he would do that.

"Don't be scared Shayna," he whispered to her.

He leaned down toward her and with his soft, but deadly, fingers he gently moved the hair off of her shoulder, exposing her throat. The veins in her neck throbbed with every beat of her heart. Right there. He thought, eyeing the biggest vein.

"This won't hurt too much." He leaned in even closer to her. "If you don't fight it."

Shayna closed her eyes tightly. This is it. She thought. This is how I am going to die. She let out a muffled cry, and tried to imagine Cain's face, so her mind would be, where she wanted it to be. Aiden's hand gripped her thigh harder.

Just get it over with! She prayed. She could feel tears escaping her closed eyes.

"Look at me," Aiden said, grabbing her face under her chin, and turning her head toward him. "Open your eyes," he demanded

Afraid of what would happen if she didn't, Shayna opened her eyes. She knew she was going to die, but wanted to make it as painless as possible. Shayna looked into Aiden's eyes. Looks truly were deceiving, and as she looked at his handsome face, she knew how ugly he was inside.

"Why are you doing this Aiden? You're not a Changeling," she said. "You don't need my blood," her voice was barely a whisper. Her throat burned from the poison he had her inhale.

Aiden's eyes became red, "I don't need your blood Shayna," he hissed, and leaned closer, "I want your blood. Your blood is so unbelievably powerful. The moment I caught scent of you, I knew, I had to have you.

Shayna felt like she would vomit. She had trusted Aiden, and the whole time he had lied to her, and betrayed her, and her father.

Aiden began laughing, "I can't believe my weak brother was able to resist you for so long," he said. He looked at Shayna, and pretended to be sympathetic, "He really did love you Shayna, but he had to go," Aiden leaned in as close as he could to Shayna, "He won't be coming back for you Princess," he said, laughing harder. "I made sure of that."

Shayna spat in Aiden's face, and slapped him. He grabbed her wrists and held her down on the bed, his red eyes piercing hers.

"It's time," he said, with a hiss.

He started to lean closer to her neck again, and out of the corner of her eye, she saw movement on the balcony. She glanced over, moving only her eyes, and beheld a pair of green and red eyes staring back at her. Her heart started beating faster. She looked back to Aiden hoping he hadn't noticed her looking at the balcony.

"Cain is going to kill you," she told Aiden in a matter of fact tone.

Aiden laughed in her face, "Shayna, Shayna, you stupid little Halfling, don't you get it? Cain is dead," he smiled at her and ran his tounge across his extened canines.

Shayna started squirming under Aiden's grasp, and finally Cain stepped into the room.

"You forgot one thing brother," Cain said.

Aiden jerked his head around in Cain's direction, growling.

Cain held up his hand showing his ring to his brother, "You forgot to take my bloodstone off of me, when you through me off that bluff."

Aiden growled louder, and Shayna could feel it vibrating in her chest.

"Impossible." Aiden said. "You're dead."

Cain stepped further into the room. "No. You thought you killed a Changeling." Cain looked at Shayna, lying trapped beneath Aiden's body, her eyes were full of fear, and hope, "I wasn't a Changling, when you thought you killed me," he told Aiden.

There was a knock at the door. Aiden hissed, and turned his head to the door, and Cain took his chance. He lunged at Aiden, knocking him across the bed, and onto the floor on the otherside.

Knock. Knock.

"Shayna, are you in there?" It was Noah.

Shayna couldn't peel her eyes away from Cain and Aiden fighting, it was like something she thought she would only see in the movies. They viciously growled at each other, and tore chunks of flesh from each others bodies. She feared that the outcome would be bad for both of them. Shayna slowly got off of the bed, and started making her way to the door. Aiden saw her, and growled. His blood red eyes locked in on her like missiles. He managed to slip away from Cain, and made a move for Shayna, grabbing a handful of her hair, and yanking her to him. Shayna screamed. Holding her, with her back to him, Aiden sank his teeth deep into her neck. He hadn't got the bulging vein he had hoped for, but he would settle for where he landed.

Cain pulled the platinum dagger out of his boot, and rushed toward Aiden with it, and stuck in deep into the middle of his back. He knew it wouldn't do any permanent damage, but he had to do whatever her could to make him release Shayna.

Aiden howled in surprise, and pain, and let Shayna's body fall to the floor. Cain dropped to his knees beside her, and scooped her up into his arms, where she would be safe. The hawk flew out of the open balcony window, just as Noah finally broke through the door. Cain held Shayna.

"I love you. I'm so sorry I let this happen," Cain told her.

Shayna returned Cain's hold tighter than ever, and smiled at him. Tears of joy and relief running down her face. Noah stood in the doorway watching the two, and seeing blood on Shayna's neck, he gasped.

"Is she okay?' he asked Cain, pointing at Shayna's neck.

Cain touched the steady trickle of blood on Shayna's neck, that was running down her collarbone and onto Aunt Mill's beautiful, elegant dress.

"He didn't have time to take any blood," Cain said, "I think he only bit her.

He looked into the ocean of blue diamonds in Shayna's eyes, and held her face in his hand. He pulled her closer to his face, and leaned her head back. His mouth opened slightly, and he moved in. This is going to be phenominal! He thought, anticipating the kiss to come.

Cain's bottom lip brushed Shayna's, and as soon as it did, Shayna's whole body stiffened, and she began frantically grabbing for Cain. A horrifying scream escaped her lips, and her face twisted, in agonizing pain.

"Shayna!" Noah and Cain both cried out.

Noah ran to the other side of them. He saw that Shayna's nose was bleeding. His stomach flipped, and he lost the french dinner he and Melina had shared, on the white carpet.

This is it. Shayna thought. I'm turning. She tried to speak but was unable to. She wanted to tell Cain, that she was sorry too. She wanted to tell him that she loved him. Her back arched, and her body started to twist in an unhumanly way.

"Shayna," his harmonic voice said, "Stay with me Shayna." She could still feel his cold touch.

"Oh my God!" She heard Noah cry.

"I love you Shayna." Shayna loved this voice, "I won't leave you, I promise."

The sound of Cain's voice remained with her, and everything else, faded away.

Epilogue

I never realized that being born immortal meant that my mortal self would have to die. When it felt like my heart was being ripped from my chest, I knew that I was dying. The last thing I saw when my heart stopped was Cain's face. His emerald green eyes were so full of sadness to see me in so much pain. He did come back for me.

It felt like my veins were on fire, and as the fire raced for my heart, I could still hear Cain telling me that he loved me. I'm going to miss him while I'm gone, but I will return…in a new beginning.

To Be Continued

Cimmerian Utopia

It doesn't matter what she was, all that matters is what she is.

Jump right back into the Born Immortal series right where Midnight Blood leaves off.

After Shayna recovers from her transformation into an immortal existance, she is left with more questions then answers and a thirst for blood that both entices Cain and frightens him.

When Aiden returns for what he claims is his, Shayna is pulled into a world that is darker then she could have ever imagined, and filled with secrets about herself and her destiny, that could change her existance forever.

Alone, and once again guarded by Aiden, Shayna is left with no choice but to trust him with her life, or die before her secrets are ever revealed.

To be released winter of 2012

Made in the USA
Charleston, SC
09 September 2012